Echoes of
Expectation:

Waiting

P. A. Farrell

ISBN: 979-8-9930004-5-9

Books by Patricia A. Farrell, Ph.D.

When You Can't Pour From an Empty Glass: CBT Skills for Exhausted Caregivers

The Little Book on Learning Big Critical Thinking Skills

The Smart Kid's Survival Guide: Making Good Choices in a Confusing World

How to Be Your Own Therapist

It's Not All in Your Head: Anxiety, Depression, Mood Swings and Multiple Sclerosis

Unfiltered: Beneath the noise of our thoughts lies the true narrative of our minds

Unfiltered Again: A behind-the-scenes look at healthcare, medicine and mental health

A Social Security Disability Psychological Claims Handbook: A simple guide to understanding your SSD claim for psychological impairments and unraveling the maze of decision-making

A Social Security Disability Psychological Claims Guidebook for Children's Benefits

The Disability Accessible US Parks in All 50 States: A Comprehensive Guide

P. A. FARRELL

Birding in the US NOW!: A birding guide for individuals with disabilities

Contents

Introduction

We spend so much of our lives waiting. Waiting for the phone to ring, for the bus to arrive, for test results, for the storm to pass. Waiting can be dull; it can be agonizing, or it can be quietly sacred. In the moments between what has ended and what is still to come, something inside us stirs.

This collection is about those spaces, the thresholds where ordinary people pause and wrestle with uncertainty, hope, or fear. Through a delayed flight, a traveler finds connection with strangers during the long night. A tired insomniac counts the drips of her coffeepot, waiting for courage to dial a number that could change everything. And even a dog named Fritzy, once labeled a failure, waits for his moment to prove what love and loyalty truly mean.

Each story asks the same question in different ways: what happens to us while we wait? Do we falter? Do we grow? Do we discover strength we didn't know we had?

These tales are brief but not small. Like the pauses in music, they give shape and meaning to what comes next. I invite you to lean into the silences, the stillness, the seconds that stretch—and discover what waits inside the waiting.

The Waiting Room

T he elevator doors opened onto the third floor with a reluctant sigh. Fluorescent lights hummed overhead, throwing their pale glow onto linoleum tiles polished thin by decades of footsteps. A sign pointed left: "Oncology." To the right: "Cardiology." Straight ahead: "Waiting Room."

Clara stepped out, clutching her handbag to her chest as though it might shield her. Her husband was in surgery two floors below. The doctors had said words she only half-heard—"procedure," "risk," "hours." They had directed her here to wait.

The room was a patchwork of chairs upholstered in tired blue fabric, with a television in the corner mumbling the news to no one in particular. Coffee percolated on a side table, its bitter scent mingling with disinfectant. The air carried the nervous rustle of magazines, the creak of shifting bodies, the silence of lives on pause.

Clara chose a chair near the window. Outside, the city went on indifferently as buses hissed, pedestrians hurried, a woman with a red umbrella laughed into her phone. Life moved. Inside, time was, as they say, molasses in January.

Across from her sat an older man in a tweed cap, hands folded over a cane. He gave her a polite nod. Beside him, a young mother tried to entertain her toddler with a stuffed rabbit, her smile stretched thin. Two teenagers slouched with earbuds in, occasionally glancing at the clock. And in the far corner, a nun held a rosary, her lips moving soundlessly.

Each person was waiting, although the reasons for their wait varied. Clara felt the weight of it, the way waiting pressed people into a strange fellowship.

The man with the cap leaned forward slightly. "First time here?"

She nodded. "My husband. Surgery."

He tapped his cane once against the floor. "My wife, too. Different kinds, though we've been here often enough to know the wallpaper by heart." His smile was wan. "You get to recognize the patterns."

Clara swallowed, unsure if she wanted to recognize anything about this place. She glanced at the clock: ten minutes gone.

The young mother dropped the rabbit, and it skidded across the floor. Clara bent quickly, retrieved it, and offered it back. The child's fingers brushed hers, sticky with candy. The mother mouthed a "thank you," her eyes bright with fatigue. For a moment, Clara felt less alone.

The nun began humming softly, a tune without words. The sound threaded through the room, weaving a quiet calm. Even the television seemed to lower its volume.

Hours stretched. People came and went, their names called by nurses in pastel-colored scrubs. The teenagers left first, muttering, "He'll text us." The man in the cap was called next; he rose slowly, tipping his hat to Clara as though she were an old friend. The young mother dozed, her child curled in a small ball against her. The nun prayed on, her presence steady as the ticking clock. Would all those prayers help, or was it merely a way to pass this horrible time lag that felt like days, not hours?

Clara pulled a book from her bag, one she had carried for weeks without opening. The same paragraph went unabsorbed after three reads. She thought of her husband's laugh, of the way he whistled while fixing the leaky faucet, and of the garden they'd meant to plant this spring. She thought of what she might have to do if the waiting ended badly. Her chest ached.

At last a nurse appeared, her expression unreadable. "Mrs. Henderson?"

Clara's heart seized. She stood, legs unsteady. The room seemed to lean with her.

"Your husband is stable," the nurse said quickly, as though she knew the importance of those first words. "The surgery went well. He's in recovery. You can see him in a little while."

Relief flooded Clara so suddenly she nearly wept. She sank back into the chair, trembling. The mother stirred awake, the nun looked up and smiled, and for an instant Clara felt that they all shared her exhale.

The waiting had ended, but the room itself remained—ready for the next wave of footsteps, the next names, the next hearts held in suspension. Clara rose, smoothing her skirt. She whispered to the nun, "Thank you for the music."

The nun touched her beads. "It helps with the waiting," she said simply.

Clara walked out into the hallway, her steps light, carrying with her the strange fellowship of those who had kept vigil together. Outside, the city still hurried, umbrellas still opened against the drizzle. But she had learned something in that third-floor room: waiting binds, even strangers, in invisible threads of hope.

The Letter That Never Came

T he first time Nora checked the mailbox after the funeral, she did it without thinking. Muscle memory pushed her down the front steps, past the azaleas, across the little oval of shade the maple spread smoothly at noon. The box's metal lip was hot. Inside, a circular for tires, a glossy postcard promising windows that would change her life, and a folded envelope addressed to "Resident." Nothing with his handwriting. She stood there a minute longer than she needed to, as if the extra sixty seconds might coax the past to catch up.

On day two, she told herself she was only checking in case there were documents from the lawyer. On day seven, she gave up the lie and admitted she was waiting for the letter he'd promised—"I'll write something for you to open after," he'd said lightly, as if "after" were a season you could plan for. "Not a goodbye. I don't believe in those. More like a… map." He had always loved maps: rivers with names like prayers, roads that braided towns to one another.

She told no one she was waiting. People were kind, but kindness had its own gravity; it pulled you toward the center of what others thought grief should look like. She attended, nodded, sent thank-you cards for casseroles that lasted into a third week and then grew little white wisps in their corners. When she couldn't sleep, she drafted articles for the website that still paid her to write about city gardens. She set timers, watered basil, and watched the stems lean toward the light. And each afternoon at one, she walked to the mailbox.

One afternoon, the mail truck stopped long enough for her to meet the carrier. He was young, probably late twenties, with a sunburn peeling along his neck and a quick, shy half-smile.

"Hi," he said, sliding envelopes in. "You're Nora, right? I'm Luis. I took over this route last month."

"I'm Nora," she said, surprised to hear her voice as though it were being used by someone else. "Do you ever—do letters ever get... lost?"

He pulled back slightly, considering. "Not often. Sometimes they're delayed. Hand-sorted stuff can take weird paths." He paused. "Are you waiting for something?"

She started to say no, then shrugged. "A letter from my husband. He... He said he was writing one. I thought it would come."

"I'm sorry," he mumbled, and his eyes didn't flinch away. "If you want, I'll watch for it. Sometimes the old office misroutes from the hospital. But it'll find you. Letters are good at that."

After he left, she wanted to believe him. She carried the junk mail inside like it mattered, stacked it on the kitchen table, and brewed tea that she forgot to drink. Her sister called, and Nora said she was fine. "You don't sound fine," her sister said with a hint of a question.

"I'm practicing."

"For what?"

"For sounding fine," Nora said, and felt, finally, the ridiculousness of it. She laughed and then cried, and her sister listened, and the day rounded a corner she hadn't known was there.

Weeks unwound. The basil erupted into green hands. Nora began seeing the neighborhood with morning eyes again: the woman on the corner walking three dachshunds like commas, the high-schooler who sat on his front steps playing a trumpet so tenderly it made the sky hold its breath. She worked, emailed clients, and taught a workshop on balcony gardens where she repeated the things she knew by heart: there is no plant that doesn't stretch toward light; moisture matters more than you think; patience is not waiting in stillness but tending while you wait.

Luis waved when he passed. Sometimes he'd pause and tell her about the old Victorian on Holden where the lady grew tomatoes in paint buckets, or the lavender hedge by the community center that bees worshiped. He was training for a marathon, he revealed one day, and she gave him a mason jar of lemon slices and salt, old runner's remedy her father had taught her. He looked stunned by the gift, as if kindness were a letter addressed to him.

"You'll get your letter," he said before he left. "I can feel it."

One Tuesday morning in September, Nora saw an envelope in the box with familiar loops on the N of her name. Her breath snagged. The envelope was cream, not white, the kind they bought for wedding invitations once when they were broke and everything felt like it would expand to fit them. Her hands shook so hard she nearly dropped it. She carried it to the kitchen like an invocation and set it on the table.

She didn't open it. Not at first. She made coffee, sat down, stood up, made toast she didn't want, cleaned the sink, sat down again. The envelope waited with the patience of a stone.

When she slid her finger under the flap, the paper released with a sound like a small sigh. Inside: a single page, not his handwriting after all, but a typed note on letterhead from the hospice where he'd died. The letter explained that patients sometimes dictated memorial messages, that his had been delayed because the volunteer who typed them had taken time off to care for her own father, then returned and found the queue longer than grief.

Nora exhaled, feeling the shape of disappointment and recognizing it as the twin of relief. The promise of his letter had been one of the last beams holding up the scaffolding of her life. She wasn't sure how to feel about its substitute—official, institutional, careful. The last paragraph was his. The nurse had typed his words exactly:

*"Nora—If this arrives, it means I didn't get to write what I wanted by hand, which is the only honest way I know. But typed words are still words. I kept thinking I had more time to make the language neat. Turns out neat is overrated. Here is my mess: I love you. You already know what to do. You taught me the way plants turn. Keep turning."

She touched the period after "turning." It was a dot on the horizon. She waited for instruction—some explicit map to grief—and felt a small anger bloom when none came. He had always been annoyingly confident that she could find roads other people missed. The confidence had irritated her when he was alive. Now it steadied her like a hand at her back.

She walked out to the porch. Across the street, the trumpet boy was practicing scales that sounded more like determination than music. The mail truck crawled down the block like a beetle with a blue uniform. She held the letter up to the light and saw nothing but paper fibers and the shadow of herself.

When Luis reached her steps, he saw the letter in her hand and smiled. "It came."

"It did," she said. "Sort of."

He frowned a question.

"It's not what I thought. But it's what I have." She handed him the hospice's envelope so he could see the return address. He nodded.

"My dad's letters came late," he said. "Even when he was around." He winced. "Sorry—that came out wrong."

"No, I understand." She folded the page back into the envelope. "He believed in maps. He believed I could find my own."

Luis shifted his bag. "When I run early, there's this moment where the sun hits the pavement and everything glows. I tell myself that's where I'm headed, even if I'm still in the dark. Maybe letters are like that."

She considered this. "Do you ever write them?"

"Letters?"

"Maps."

He laughed. "Only with my feet." He hesitated, then added, "If you ever want company on a short run, I go slow on Thursdays."

"I garden slow on Thursdays," she said. "But you can stop for lemonade."

They shared a small, conspiratorial smile—the kind you give a neighbor when you've both decided to live in the same place on purpose. After he left, she took the letter back inside and pinned it to the corkboard above the desk where she wrote about how to coax life from clay pots.

Autumn followed its own map. The trumpet boy learned a blues riff that made the stray cats pause in their prowling. The woman with the dachshunds added a fourth dog, an exclamation point. Leaves flared, then fell. On Thursdays, Luis ran past and waved, pink-cheeked and grinning, and sometimes paused long enough to stretch by the maple and accept a glass of lemonade that tasted the way the word "keep" might taste if it were a fruit. So strange, but so true.

The letter became less a destination and more a landmark she passed each day. She no longer checked the mailbox with the clenched expectation that had made her hands ache. She still went, but often she returned with nothing and felt nothing more than the pleasant disappointment of rain that never quite arrives. She started writing letters of her own: to friends she hadn't seen in years, to her sister, to a woman she found through a grief forum whose husband had left a house full of model ships that gathered dust like minor storms. Nora wrote of basil and balconies, of waiting that didn't feel like punishment but like breath taken before a note.

One evening, while trimming back the browned stems to make room for winter rosemary, Nora noticed an old envelope tucked into the porch swing's slat, yellow and brittle. Her name was on it in his unmistakable hand—he always made the N flourish like a flag. Unsteady, she slipped a fingernail under the flap. Inside, a card with a photograph of a road vanishing into pines.

"If you find this late, that's okay," the note read in his hand. *"I hid it because I was afraid of being too heavy, too soon. There's nothing in here you don't know. But sometimes knowing needs to be said out loud: You have always been braver than I am. Wait as long as you need, then go. I'll meet you in whatever you choose. Maps are made by walking."*

She laughed, a sound that startled the sparrows into lifting. Of course he had hidden a letter where she would sit when she needed to sit the most. Of course his words were a door, not a destination. She pressed the card to her chest and felt her heartbeat knock against it like someone asking to be let out.

The next day at one, she went to the mailbox anyway. Habit had become a kind of prayer, and prayers are a kind of map too. There was nothing inside but a flyer for gutter cleaning and a handwritten note on a blue sticky square: "Thurs lemonade? – L"

She grinned and wrote back on the corner of the flyer: "Always. – N" She folded the reply so it wouldn't cut his fingers when he reached in. Then she took the hospice note and the hidden card, pinned them side by side above her desk, and began an essay titled "How to Water the Basil When You Are Waiting." She wrote about light, and turning, and the way letters sometimes arrive early and sometimes late and sometimes exactly when you've stopped looking for them.

When she finished, she didn't wait to send it. She clicked "submit," then walked to the porch and sat on the swing, letting it carry her back and forth between what was and what would be. Somewhere down the block, the trumpet began a melody she almost recognized. It would come to her, she thought, if she waited without clutching.

Inside, on the corkboard, the two letters waited without urgency—the one that had finally come and the one that had been here all along. She looked at them once more, then let the screen door hush closed behind her and stepped into the sunlight.

The Clockmaker's Apprentice

The shop smelled of oil and lemon polish, a scent that clung to the wainscoting and to the cuffs of anyone who worked there long enough. On autumn afternoons, light came through the front window in slices, laying bright bars across the glass cases where pocket watches slept like coins. The town's clocks—mantel, carriage, bracket, and cuckoo made a crowded choir, each voice insisting on its own precise truth. Some chimed the hour like a proclamation; others whispered it like a secret.

Theo apprenticed under Mr. Anselm, who had been repairing time for as long as anyone could remember. People brought him their clocks when they ran fast, slow, or not at all; he returned them with faces newly serene. He wore a magnifying loupe that left a pale circle around his right eye, the only part of him the sun touched during the winter months. He laughed rarely but kindly and never hurried. "Rushing," he said, "is a lie we tell the hour. It doesn't believe us."

Theo learned first to listen. Each mechanism spoke in a dialect—the long sway of a regulator, the nervous tick of a travel alarm, and the stern cadence of a tower escapement. He sorted tiny screws in teacups and cleaned spring barrels with a patience he had not known he possessed. Patience grew in him like a second heartbeat.

But patience, he discovered, is not the same as waiting. Waiting had weight. The townspeople brought that weight with them: a widow whose kitchen clock had stopped the morning after the funeral and would not start; a grocer whose father's pocket watch lost three minutes every day, the exact number he'd been late to the birth of his only child; and a girl who saved for months to buy a watch for her brother deploying overseas. They wanted accuracy, yes, but also absolution. Theo could polish, adjust, re-bush, and re-pin, but absolution eluded him.

One day a man arrived holding a small walnut bracket clock, the kind that had once sat on mantels when houses believed in mantels. He looked exhausted in the way serious men do when they decide to trust strangers. "It was my mother's," he said. "It stopped at eleven eighteen on the night she died. I thought it was superstition, but every time I wind it now, it runs until exactly eleven eighteen and stops."

Mr. Anselm nodded gravely. "We'll see to it."

After the customer left, Theo leaned in. "Haunted?"

"Clocks are haunted by us," the old man said, half-smiling. "Open it."

Theo lifted the back and found, beneath the usual architecture of plates and gears, a sliver of something folded into the space under the bell. Paper? No—thin vellum, nearly translucent. Words in a crabbed hand: *I will wait for you, even where waiting is not needed.*

He felt the hair on his arms rise. "Someone wrote this?"

"Someone always writes something," Mr. Anselm murmured. "Most hides are less tidy."

They restored the clock: cleaned the pallet faces, trued the crutch, reset the suspension spring. At eleven eighteen, it ticked past its old arrest, unbothered, and kept going as if it had never learned to stop.

"Why eleven eighteen?" Theo asked.

"Because someone needed it to stop then," the old man said, "until someone else needed it not to." He said the words like a recipe, practiced and plain.

Weeks turned into months. Theo learned to hear the difference between impatience and urgency, between neglect and wear. He learned that some people wanted their clocks righted and others wanted their memories repaired. He learned that Mr. Anselm kept two notebooks: one for parts and hours billed, another filled with short entries, each beginning with a time and ending with a sentence that sounded like a riddle.

3:07—returned a minute to the grieving.

9:52—kept the promise for the sailor.

1:14—held the breath until the child arrived.

Theo read over his shoulder once and felt as if he'd peeked into a church. The old man closed the book slowly, not angry. "Some records you keep only to remember that they're not yours to keep."

December arrived with a weather of clocks—late dawns, early dusk, gusts that rattled the shop's bell. The town square's tower clock, which Mr. Anselm tended, began to lag. By Christmas, it had surrendered seven minutes. People complained. Trains didn't wait for sentiment. The mayor sent a note with his heavy seal. "The town needs its time," he wrote, as if time were grain to be taxed.

On the coldest morning of the year, Mr. Anselm climbed the narrow iron ladder inside the tower to the room where the great movement lived. He stood beside the escape wheel, hand on the pendulum, and listened with his eyes closed as if to a sick friend. "Do you hear it?" he said to Theo. "The weight isn't falling right."

Theo heard only the usual: tick, tock, a breath between. "We can add weight," he offered.

"Weight won't fix what waiting has done," the old man said, and smiled in a way that made Theo uneasy. "Here—fetch the small tin from my coat."

Inside the tin were three tiny vials stoppered with wax. Each held something that looked like dust caught in light.

"What is it?" Theo asked.

"Minutes," Mr. Anselm said simply. "Held ones. People give them to clocks without knowing. Every time someone waits—truly waits, with intention—the minute doesn't pass so much as it settles. A good clock catches some. A better keeper learns how to put them back."

Theo laughed once, because the notion delighted him before it frightened him. "You're teasing."

The old man's face didn't change. "Take the first vial. When I lift the pendulum, pour this onto the anchor. Slowly."

The tower room smelled of iron and cold. Theo did as he was told, and the dust—if dust it was—clung to the oiled metal and then seemed to vanish into it. The pendulum took on a slightly wider arc, as if a breath had opened in its chest. The escape wheel's tick brightened. Theo checked his watch. The tower clock matched it to the second.

"How—" he began.

"Because the town has been waiting," Mr. Anselm said. "For spring. For verdicts. For letters. Waiting collects. The clock was heavy with held minutes and then suddenly starving without them. We returned a portion."

They descended, shoulders whitened by the tower's flour of dust. In the square, a woman looked up, clapped once, and said, "About time," and then laughed at her own joke. Theo felt taller and smaller at the same moment.

That night, Mr. Anselm coughed hard enough to lean against the workbench. The cough rattled like a loose screw in a tin. He waved Theo off. "I've outwaited more winters than I had any right to. Help me close."

They wound the day's finished clocks and put blankets over the glass cases like goodnight kisses. Theo turned the sign to CLOSED and noticed, tucked between the doorjamb and the frame, an envelope addressed in the old man's hand. "For when I'm not," it read. He pretended not to see it.

The next morning, Mr. Anselm didn't come down. Theo made tea and brought it up the crooked back staircase. The old man sat on the bed, dressed but not laced, looking at the window as if it were a far-off shore.

"I dreamed of the tower clock," he said. "We were both on time." He smiled. "You'll open the envelope now."

Theo obeyed. Inside was a short letter and a key so small it looked like a child's. The letter said: *There is a drawer you haven't found. This key opens it. I never told you because telling isn't the same as teaching. Waiting is a teacher. When you are ready, unlock the drawer and decide.*

The drawer was hidden beneath the workbench, behind a false panel. Theo had cleaned around it a hundred times without noticing. He turned the tiny key and pulled the door open. Inside lay a single vial, larger than the others, its dust dense as late afternoon. On its wax: *For the promise we couldn't keep.*

Theo understood and feared that he understood. He climbed the stairs two at a time. "I won't," he said to the old man, already crying.

"You might," the old man said in a hushed tone. "And if you do, you'll do it because you must, not because you can."

"I can give it to you," Theo said. "A held minute. Maybe more."

"A held minute is not a spared life," Mr. Anselm said. "It's a kept promise. Use it to keep one."

The town's bells marked noon, then one. Snow began, a veil that brightened the air. Theo sat beside the bed. They talked about trivial things: the uneven hinge on the second case, the sailor who never came back for his clock, the taste of oranges. At two o'clock, Mr. Anselm closed his eyes and breathed shallowly. At three, he did not wake.

When the undertaker left, Theo locked the door and turned every clock in the shop to the same hour: three. He wound none of them. The room filled with a silence that was somehow not empty—a hum of held minutes, he thought, or else only grief's tinnitus.

After dark, he lit the lamp over the bench and took out the vial. He held it up. In the glow, the dust looked like motes, but when he tilted it a certain way he saw other things: the widow's kitchen, the grocer's guilt, the girl's letter to her brother she had never mailed. He saw how waiting could be a kind of love, not a vacancy but a presence.

He broke the wax. The smell was not of dust but of rain after a long summer. He carried the vial to the tower, the streets muffled by snow, the town so quiet he could hear his own breath syncing with his stride. He climbed until his legs shook and stood again beside the great pendulum. He thought of promises: I'll be there; I won't leave; I'll wait.

He poured the minute onto the anchor and felt the whole tower inhale. The pendulum's arc widened. The escapement asked and answered, asked and answered, a catechism of motion. Outside, the hands jumped forward the smallest fraction and then settled. Somewhere below, a child on a sled laughed, the sound carried into the room like a ribbon.

Theo walked back through the square. At the shop door, he paused. He had not used the minute to turn back any clock. He had used it to keep the promise the town had made to itself again and again without words: that in the worst weather, a light would still be on; that in the steepest night, the hours would still be counted; that waiting, shared, becomes less lonely. He had spent the minute to hold that promise one more day.

In the months that followed, Theo learned the rest of the craft. He mended teeth on wheels and replaced worn pivots. He wrote in the second notebook with a hand that surprised him by becoming the old man's: *7:41—returned a breath for the midwife. 12:03—caught the silence for the soldier.* He discovered that the town gave minutes without realization and that his job was to notice and to put them where they could do good. It was not wizardry so much as a stewardship.

On the first day of spring, he wound the tower clock and felt, through the key, the town turning toward light. He locked the door of the tower and stood in the square watching the hands move. People glanced up, nodded, and went about their lives. The hour struck. Somewhere, a widow's kitchen clock steadied. Somewhere, a grocer forgave himself three minutes. Somewhere, a girl posted a letter. And in the shop window, his reflection stood not as a boy but as a man holding a loupe to his eye, patient with the hour.

The clocks around him agreed. Waiting, they said in their many voices, is not emptiness. It is keeping. It is the place where promises are held until they can be given back.

The Bus Stop in Winter

The wind bit at her cheeks, sharp as glass, as Clara tucked her scarf tighter and stamped her boots against the icy pavement.The bus stop offered little shelter—just a plastic bench glazed with frost and a tilted sign that seemed to lean in sympathy.

Every weekday morning she came here. And every weekday morning, the bus was late.

The other passengers were bundled shapes, their breath puffing in clouds. A man in a neon safety vest rubbed his hands, muttering about frozen pipes. A student scrolled on her phone, thumbs darting, earbuds sealed against the world. An older woman clutched a shopping cart, its wheels squeaking when she shifted.

Clara knew them by habit if not by name. Strangers connected through waiting.

Today, though, something in her chest hummed differently. Maybe it was the dream she'd had the night before, where her late grandmother whispered, "Patience, my girl. Something's coming." Or maybe it was the job interview she had that morning, which she kept secret for fear of jinxing it.

The cold wrapped around her like a vest.She imagined the bus was more than transport. It was a possibility, carrying her away from the monotony of part-time shifts and hollow evenings. She needed this bus.

Minutes dragged. The digital display above the stop flickered, then froze.

"Figures," muttered the man in the safety vest. "It quits on you when you need it most."

Clara surprised herself by smiling. "Maybe it's just resting."

The man chuckled, shaking his head.

Silence fell again, but softer now. Clara watched her breath spiral into the air, wondering if hope was just that—something fragile you exhaled, waiting for it to linger.

The student suddenly sighed. "Exam today. If I miss it, I fail the class." Her voice cracked slightly, the bravado gone.

The older woman patted her gloved hand. "It'll come, dear. Buses always do. Not on time, but they come." Her cart's wheels squeaked again, oddly cheerful in the quiet.

Clara realized that everyone here was waiting not just for a bus, but for something bigger: relief, progress, proof that the world kept moving.

Snow fell, slowly at first, then in thick, white curtains that blurred the road. The group huddled closer under the flimsy shelter, united against the storm. Clara felt the hum in her chest again—like maybe the waiting wasn't empty but alive with possibility.

"Remember when snow days were magic?" she said aloud, surprising herself.

The student glanced up, grinning. "Yeah. Now they're just stress."

The older woman laughed, but briefly. "Back then, it meant cocoa and sledding. Now it's just shoveling and wet socks."

For a moment, the stop filled with laughter, misty breath mingling in the air like a minor rebellion against winter.

Suddenly, there were headlights in the distance. A bus.

They all straightened. But as it neared, its sign read: "Out of Service." It roared past, spraying slush, and vanished.

A groan rippled through the group.

Clara's stomach twisted. Time ticked on, her interview inching closer. Was this the universe laughing?

She looked down at her boots, snow-crusted on the laces, and thought of her grandmother again. Patience, my girl.

The student's voice broke her thoughts. "I don't think I can wait anymore." She turned to leave, shoulders slumped.

Clara reached out, gently catching her sleeve. "Stay. It'll come."

The girl hesitated. Then nodded.

Hope felt contagious.

The snow thickened, erasing the world in white. And then—faint at first, then stronger—the rumble of another engine. The shape of a bus materialized like a promise through the snowstorm. Its sign glowed: "Downtown."

Cheers, actual cheers, rose from the group.

As the doors hissed open, Clara stepped aboard, heart racing. She thought of the interview waiting downtown, of her grandmother's voice, and of how waiting could feel endless until suddenly, the thing you needed appeared.

The bus smelled of wet coats and diesel, but to Clara it smelled like hope. She slid into a seat, snowflakes melting on her scarf, and let herself believe—maybe, just maybe—this was the start of something new.

Behind her, the older woman chuckled. "See? Told you. Buses always come."

Clara smiled and looked out the window as the bus pulled into the whiteness. Waiting wasn't just passing time—it was the space where hope lived, stubborn and shimmering, even in the cold.

Silent Between Us Now

Under the sun that shines relentlessly on California, Elena and Stewart Samuels, at 78 and 81 years of age, force their squeaking, worn, and rusting shopping cart through the abandoned Los Angeles River's concrete spillway.

In contrast to the distinguished look they have in Brentwood, today their attire includes a 'UFO' hat from Bloomingdale's in 1985 and a bow tie that Stewart still stubbornly wears with his floral-print suspenders. They're here, dressed down, and in the dried riverbed, on a treasure hunt, a testament to Elena's unyielding determination.

Elena holds a crumpled, hand-drawn map in her hand like a general preparing to embark on a military campaign. Stewart, who is initially reluctant and complaining about his new dentures, is unable to resist his wife's enthusiasm. Their partnership has been like this for 52 years of marriage—her wild inspirations, his reluctant participation, and the surprise and joy they find in each adventure, which is evident to anyone who sees them. Their sporadic hoots, giggles, and smiling faces are all on display for any passing witness.

Sound investments have enabled a comfortable retirement and the opportunity to pursue enjoyment and fulfillment in their leisure years.

Now, an eccentric elderly couple's adventure is going to become more profound, connecting lost childhood dreams to an unexpected future, bringing together generations divided by age but united by the universal thrill of discovery.

The cart's wheels squeak, echoing off the graffiti-filled cement walls. Every bump and crack they traverse causes their seeming worldly possessions, which include a small suitcase, a broken umbrella, and Stewart's prized 1940s radio, to rattle.

Elena wears a faded yellow sundress, practical walking shoes, and her wide-brimmed hat to shield her face from the skin-drying sunlight. She tells Stewart that a woman must take care of her skin in the sun. Stewart rolls his eyes. Under the hat and neck scarf is a porcelain-like, barely lined face, a tribute to a high-priced plastic surgeon.

Elena bought the hat at Bloomingdale's in 1985, and she will not give it up. Stewart chides her every now and then by saying, "You look like a UFO made of straw." But she soldiers on. As usual on these adventures, he's wearing his characteristic bow tie and floral-print suspenders and maintains his dignity even as sweat darkens his local Goodwill store short-sleeved shirt.

They are not homeless, far from it. Their Brentwood home is worth millions. Today, they are on a mission. Elena read in the LA Times about legendary treasure that was supposed to be buried in the riverbed during the last flood years ago. After five decades of marriage, Stewart knows better than to argue. He knows what happens when Elena gets "that look" in her eyes. So, he gives in and keeps his thoughts to himself, avoiding an argument that he knows will come.

The sun gives them no relief as they walk past the rusted beer cans, bits of clothing, and soil scattered on the ground. Uncharacteristically kicking a can aside, Elena consults her hand-drawn map, which she made from newspaper clippings and local folklore. Stewart continues to mutter about his new dentures, but his complaints lack conviction or a willing audience. Deep down, he is enjoying these adventures, though he would never admit it.

They walk under bridges where graffiti artists have painted massive protest messages, abstractions, and disturbing murals. Elena stops to admire the work and offers her art criticism. She says, "That one looks like your cousin Sylvia after she tried hot yoga," as she points to an abstract face. Stewart cannot help but laugh—it does.

A group of teenage skateboarders rolls by, initially snickering at the elderly couple as they work together to free their cart from a rut. But, their laughter turns into curiosity after they stop, and Stewart tells them about the treasure hunt. Suddenly, they are helping the Samuels and joining in the search. This unexpected turn of events bridges generations, and the power of shared experiences becomes clear.

A specific spot, marked with a faded red X, appears on Elena's map. The skateboarders assist them in excavating years of accumulated rusted cans, together with old clothing bits, tree twigs, and hopeless soil sediment. As the sun sets, long, grey shadows creep across the concrete canyon. Stewart, astonished by his recall of his father's accounts, explains the 1938 flood to the teens.

Elena has heard his stories before, so she uses her trowel and strikes something solid. The boys leave Stewart and gather near her as she removes the dirt. A loaf-sized metal container with a rusted exterior and packed dirt accumulation sits before them.

The teenagers record their discovery with cell phone cameras as Stewart assists Elena in opening the metal box. The baseball cards inside the container hazily appear through thick, yellowed wax paper. Stewart's hand trembles. A time capsule contains the complete

Goudey and Diamond Stars card sets from 1934 to 1938. "Unbelievable," he thinks to himself.

Elena suddenly breaks into uncontrollable laughter because the name "Property of Stewart Samuels, 1938" is written inside the box lid. The collection wasn't destroyed in the flood.

Stewart stares in disbelief. The flood from 1938 took his baseball card collection when he was eight years old, and he forgot he owned it. He realizes they are witnessing something exceptional, and the teenagers help the couple place the box into the shopping cart.

The couple walk home hand in hand; the skateboarders transport the box in the shopping cart behind them. One of the teenagers has already checked his phone to discover that the total worth of the collection exceeds half a million dollars. Stewart continues to shake his head as he laughs, still in disbelief.

"You knew all along, didn't you?" he asks Elena.

She adjusts her UFO hat and smiles mysteriously. "I might have run into your sister last month. The discussion was about a box containing baseball cards and a flood event."

"Fifty-two years of marriage, and you still surprise me," Stewart says, squeezing her hand.

She pushes up her nose in a telltale facial gesture. "Someone needs to keep you on your toes."

The couple donates the collection to a deserving institution— a children's museum. Stewart selects one special baseball card for each of their skateboarding friends, and, as these cards are valued at $500 each, it provides an ideal start for collecting. Recognized by the local community, Elena and Stewart are celebrities because they united different generations through an unexpected afternoon adventure.

In the following months, Stewart teaches local children about baseball history, and the Samuels' driveway becomes a regular gathering place every Sunday morning, where Elena provides homemade cup-cakes and assorted beverages for everyone who comes.

Still, Elena constantly wears a different UFO hat from Goodwill as she pours lemonade and shares amusing stories about her and Stew-art's life, like how they got the seeds for those purple tomatoes in their garden.

The retired shopping cart stands in the garage next to their Mer-cedes-Benz. In the basement, the tattered Goodwill outfits, carefully boxed, wait for another adventure, should Elena discover one.

Dust to Dust

It's time. They're taking her away now, wrapped in that awful black bag that I can't seem to take my attention away from, and that rivets me now. How quickly it all passed. For 63 years, I saw her life unfolding: her hair thinning, widow's tears falling, and children growing and moving on. But now, strangers stomp through her frail sanctuary, speaking in loud, irreverent voices about "estate sales" and "market value." I hate all of it with all the hate anyone like me can muster. But what can I do? I am a confined prisoner, and my voice will never be heard in her behalf or even for others. Mute, as I am, I still have the ability to think, if only for myself, and never to be heard by others.

If they only knew what lived behind my glass, nestled against my simple wooden molding. But it's just as well. None of them seems to notice. I am invisible to them, as I was never to her. To tell you the truth, I don't want to be recognized, I don't want to be touched, and I don't want to be moved—but I have no choice. They make all the decisions now. I am an object to them. It was never like that for her, and for that I will always be grateful.

One of her nephews runs his dirty fingers along my frame. His greasy fingers leave prints on the glass protecting my faded garden scene—his evident disrespect is obvious. I want to pull away and shudder as he touches me. But I can't.

This man has visited twice in twenty years. Now he comes to collect his reward, undeserving as it is. Twenty years of lonely Christmases, no Thanksgiving dinners, and holidays without a call, a card, or a token bouquet of flowers. She'd baked cookies for the neighborhood kids as though she didn't have a care in the world. Tollhouse, oatmeal, and ginger snaps were her specialty, and the kids loved them. They'd knock on the door and jump up and down when she opened it, holding a big bowl full of fresh, warm cookies. The air filled with shouts of "Cookies! Cookies!" Eager hands dived in and pulled out prizes to tuck into pockets for later.

It's quiet as the man surveys the room. Looking again, he sees only a worthless reproduction—pink peonies on a weathered lattice, the print that filled every grandmother's house years ago. The expression on his face is unmistakable, and his lip quivers with disgust, yet I remain unaffected. She and I shared so many wonderful years together; he can do nothing to destroy those memories.

"This one's trash," he yells to the estate agent, going through everything in the next room and noting valuations on his pad. "Nobody wants this dated stuff anymore. Get it out of here quickly so we can get this up for sale." His estimate illustrates his ignorance, and if I could, I would chuckle, but I will not give that to him. He deserves nothing.

The agent notes, "Alright, toss that one in the dumpster." This is reminiscent of Sherman's march to the sea during the Civil War, only this war is in a woman's home, and there will be no burning. The agent meticulously examines her treasured possessions, deciding whether to sell, destroy, or give away.

I've guarded her secret since that night when she slipped it behind me with her old yet somehow fresh and smooth hands. Her breath fogged my glass as she whispered, "Keep it safe," as she gave me a delicate tap. The weight of it has pressed against my back ever since, through countless dustings and wall relocations, including the time her youngest granddaughter almost knocked me down while practicing cartwheels. That was the last time a child's laughter filled these rooms with joyful abandon. So long ago, and she cherished that laughter and wished for more of it, but they never came. The echoes of their laughter live only within me now.

The dumpster pile grows. They add her crocheted doilies, plastic-covered photo albums, and a collection of tiny souvenir bells—a lifetime dismissed as worthless by those who should treasure it.

Night falls. I hang crooked now, knocked askew by careless workmen's elbows as they pushed and pulled furniture out the front door. In the morning, they'll return to finish clearing all these years of memories. Soon, I'll be carried out with the trash, my secret still entombed like some Egyptian treasure behind these worthless peonies.

But wait—what's that? A shadow moves below. Someone's breaking in through the kitchen window. The nephew? No, too small, too quick. A thief, drawn by rumors of valuable antiques still unclaimed?

Footsteps approach. A flashlight beam sweeps the walls and finds me. Young, small hands lift me down with surprising gentleness. It's the paper girl who used to read to her every Wednesday afternoon while she dozed in her recliner. The one who listened to her stories about the war, lost love, and secrets that must be kept.

The girl's fingers work skillfully and sure at my simple cardboard backing. She knows. Somehow, she knows. Did she tell her?

I feel the weight shift as she removes it. It's not jewels, money, or anything glittering—just three onion-skin sheets, the kind used during WWII, pressed together with a thin piece of yellow ribbon—letters that could destroy three families, expose seven decades of lies, and unravel a web of careful silence.

The girl tucks the letters into her jacket, hanging me perfectly straight again. Tomorrow, I'll be tossed into the dumpster, light as air, my duty done. They'll never know I was anything but a worthless print, slowly fading into obscurity, taking one last secret with me into the dark. I'll be thrown out without a second thought, but I'll know her secret is safe with the paper girl, and it will be enough.

The Last Train North

The station was nearly deserted, its cavernous hall echoing with the sound of a single broom scraping across the tiled floor. A bitter wind slid through the cracked doors, carrying with it the scent of coal smoke and winter. Above, the clock struck eleven-thirty, its hands inching toward midnight. In thirty minutes, the last northbound train would depart.

Eleanor sat on a wooden bench near the far end of the platform, her suitcase resting against her calves. The suitcase was old—her husband's once, the corners worn smooth from decades of business trips. He had been gone for five years now, yet the case remained, stubbornly whole, as if waiting to be useful again. Tonight, it held her entire life: two dresses, a framed photograph, and a folded letter she hadn't dared read in full.

She had been waiting for months. Waiting for the courage, waiting for the right time, waiting for something—anything—to push her past the threshold of hesitation. The train north represented escape, but also risk. Beyond lay a cottage offered by her sister, a quieter life, maybe even peace. But leaving meant closing the door on the town where every street corner still whispered her name.

A man approached, his steps uncertain on the icy platform. He was tall, wrapped in a long coat, his hat pulled low. He lowered himself onto the bench beside her with a grunt. For a moment they sat in silence, watching their breath mingle with the cold.

"Cold night for waiting," he said finally, voice gravelly with age.

She offered a faint smile. "Seems most nights are cold when you're waiting."

He chuckled softly, then nodded toward her suitcase. "Heading north?"

"I haven't decided."

His eyes narrowed. "Last train leaves at midnight. After that, you'll have nothing but the long walk home."

She folded her hands over her lap. "Home isn't much of a home anymore."

The man leaned back, staring at the ceiling's iron beams. "Funny thing about trains. They don't care if you're ready. They arrive, they leave. It's us who make the waiting unbearable."

Eleanor glanced at him. There was something in his tone, a weary familiarity, as though he'd once stood where she was now. She wanted to ask, but before she could, the loudspeaker crackled, announcing the final boarding call in thirty minutes. The sound echoed like a judgment.

Her heart tightened. She pulled the folded letter from her coat pocket. The paper was yellowed, the ink faded. It was the last note her husband had written before he died—unfinished, found tucked in a book on his nightstand. She had read the first line over and over: "If you find this, know that I wanted you to keep living." But she had never turned the page. Tonight, she thought perhaps she might.

The man noticed, tilting his head. "Words can be heavier than any suitcase."

She looked down. "He wanted me to go on. But I stayed. I kept waiting for... I don't even know what anymore."

The man smiled sadly. "Maybe you've been waiting for permission you already have."

The whistle of the incoming train pierced the night. Steam rose as the engine lumbered into view, its great bulk glowing under the station lamps. A handful of passengers shuffled closer, their steps hurried. The platform came alive with motion, though sparse, like the last embers of a dying fire.

Eleanor stood, clutching the suitcase. Her legs trembled. She took a step forward, then stopped. "What if it's a mistake?" she whispered.

The man rose beside her, steadying her with a hand on her arm. His grip was strong, reassuring. "The only mistake," he said, "is waiting so long the train leaves without you."

She turned toward him fully for the first time. His face was lined, weathered, yet kind. His eyes, though, struck her most—they were the same hazel shade as her husband's. For a heartbeat, she swore she saw him standing there, urging her onward.

She gasped. "Who are you?"

The man tipped his hat with a faint smile. "Just someone who's caught too many trains, and missed more than I should have." Then he stepped back, fading into the thin crowd.

The conductor's call rang out: "Last call! Northbound train departing in five minutes!"

Eleanor's pulse hammered. She lifted the letter, finally opening it. The second line revealed itself: "*When the time comes, don't be afraid to leave the station. I'll be with you, wherever you go.*"

Tears welled in her eyes. She pressed the letter to her chest, then looked at the waiting train. Its doors yawned open, warm light spilling onto the icy platform. For once, the waiting ended. She moved forward, each step firm, her suitcase steady in her hand.

She climbed aboard, finding a seat by the window. The train lurched, then rolled forward with a deep groan of steel. As the station blurred behind her, she glimpsed the man once more, standing alone on the platform, lifting his hand in farewell. Or perhaps it was only her imagination, one final gift of memory.

Either way, she was moving at last. The last train north had carried her beyond waiting, into whatever life remained. And for the first time in years, Eleanor felt safe and happy.

Calendar Girl

The floor beneath Fred became slippery with metal shavings as he moved between the operating lathes. The work order with grease stains in his pocket displayed the custom-made alternator mount for his 1967 Shelby which collected dust in his garage. The February sunlight passing through the dirty shop windows created sparks from Johnson's metal grinder, which operated in the corner.

The calendar displayed itself between the bandsaw and drill press, where oil-stained fingers had bent its pages throughout the months. Miss July. Her auburn hair reflected sunlight through the air to become a golden and copper-colored spectacle. The green eyes of the woman locked onto him while her smile revealed all the hidden secrets he had ever concealed.

The glossy page made Fred's hand shake while he attempted to touch it. The machinery sounds faded into the background as his heart pounded in his ears.

"Johnson." His voice cracked. He took a deep breath to speak again before saying, "Johnson!"

The grinder stopped producing its loud whining sound. Johnson removed his safety glasses to reveal dark circles under his eyes. "What?"

Fred pointed at the calendar page. "Her. Who is she?"

Johnson examined the calendar page before turning his attention to Fred "Midwest Tools includes these calendars in its supplier packages every December."

Fred used his phone to take a picture of the calendar page. "Her name. Where did they discover her?

Fred sat at his home computer with his body bent forward. The blue light from the screen created dark shadows on his face while he ran the photo through multiple reverse image search platforms. Nothing. The image became so enlarged that individual pixels appeared while he searched for any signs of watermarks and photographer credits and agency logos. The bottom of the image displayed "Midwest Tools, July 2023" in tiny letters.

He pressed the redial button on his phone with his index finger.

The marketing department answered his call, so he asked to speak with them about the 2023 calendar and specifically about Miss July. I understand your privacy rules, yet I would like to know the name of the modeling agency that worked with her.

The dial tone hummed in response.

His social media feeds became filled with people sharing the same photo under the caption "Seeking this model—an urgent business opportunity." The comments section received a flood of responses which included:

"Creepy much?"

"Someone call the police."

"I met this person during my college years, but it turns out to be a different individual."

The private investigator's office had a strong smell of old coffee and cigarette smoke. The three weeks of his savings money vanished into a single manila envelope.

The PI called him on his phone.

The image was created by artificial intelligence technology. AI. The system processed the image through all accessible recognition platforms.

A hollow sound echoed through his kitchen when Fred tried to laugh. "Bullshit. The way light touches her hair reveals her true nature. Those eyes...

The call ended without warning.

The key struck against metal while he stood in the darkened space. The workshop remained empty while Johnson's machines stood like inactive titans in slumber. Fred ripped the calendar pages from their binding as he removed the entire publication.

The walls of his apartment disappeared under a mountain of printed materials and agency portfolios and photo comparisons. The Shelby remained untouched while his boss sent multiple emails and his friends left him numerous voicemails which he failed to answer.

A 3 AM scan of the high-resolution image revealed something important to him. A studio appeared in the window reflection which revealed itself to be located behind her. A photographer. A logo on their sleeve.

"Stellar Studios, Milwaukee,"

The purple sky of dawn approached as Fred drove his car toward the converted warehouse building. Through the enormous windows he saw studio lighting equipment and backdrop screens and cameras.

A woman operated studio lights with skilled movements as she worked. Her auburn hair showed signs of gray streaks. She wore casual clothing and he wondered if her eyes remained the same.

The doorbell chimed. She turned.

That smile.

Fred took a deep breath before saying, "The calendar shoot took place in July 2023."

She placed the light meter on the floor. "1978, actually." She ran her fingers along the edge of the camera, which sat beside her. "The AI system gets scanned images, which lets it create new models with different looks and features each year. With five hundred dollars, they generate an endless supply of flawless female models."

Fred gripped the rolled calendar tightly in his pocket while thinking about the woman. "But you're..." She pointed at the walls to show him. The walls displayed industrial photographs, where photographers had transformed machinery into artistic masterpieces. Currently, she worked on catalog projects, which include equipment, tooling, and parts documentation.

The calendar escaped from Fred's grasp as he looked at Miss July, who displayed her perfect empty face from the floor. Cynthia used her photography skills to find beauty in industrial objects, which she displayed through her images of chrome and steel and rust and durability.

Cynthia pointed to a collection of photographs, which she called her genuine portfolio. The real one.

The new collection at Cynthia's gallery exhibition attracted a crowd during its opening event. As a photographer, she used precise lighting to transform industrial equipment parts into flowing hair shadows and created softness in steel objects. The major attraction of this photograph was a calendar on a shop wall shown through a damaged glass window.

Fred faced the artwork before him before he turned to go. The need for work at Shelby's shop combined with his fresh understanding of how light interacts with metal objects and the genuine value of used items was something he had to attend to now.

The wall of Johnson's shop still displayed Miss July, although she now appeared dull and lifeless because she existed only as printed ink and computer code.

The Wedding Singer

Fairy lights, satin bows, and a chandelier that had likely seen better centuries glistened in the hall. Like bees, guests buzzed around the bar, their perfumes and colognes clashing in a war of scents. At the edge of it all, clutching a microphone with damp palms, stood Tony, Wedding singer. Thirty-nine. Slightly balding. Wearing a tuxedo rented for the third time that month.

Tony had been doing this gig for years, sliding between receptions, anniversaries, and retirement parties with the same smile. "Unforgettable," "At Last," and the occasional request for "Sweet Caroline." He was the soundtrack of other people's joy, a jukebox with a thinning hairline. His life was measured in setlists, not milestones.

This wedding was no different, or so he thought. The bride's uncle had already heckled him for mispronouncing "Schwartzkopf," the flower girl had spilled apple juice on the monitor, and the DJ's equipment had fried mid-toast.

Tony was the stopgap. He strummed the first chords of "Can't Help Falling in Love," his voice carrying through the hall like a prayer stitched with nerves.

Halfway through the song, his eyes landed on the bride. She was radiant, of course, but what caught him wasn't her smile; it was the way she looked at her new husband. Unwavering, luminous, the kind of gaze Tony hadn't seen in years. Maybe ever. He faltered on a lyric, caught between envy and wonder. The audience didn't notice, but Tony did. Would he ever have that moment? Time was passing, and no prospects were in sight.

The crack in his voice was his heart reminding him of its own silence.

Between sets, he sat by the fake ficus, sipping flat ginger ale. An older woman plopped into the chair beside him. She was wearing a hat that looked like it had eaten a bird. "You're good," she said, eyes twinkling. "But you sing like a man who's lost something."

Tony blinked. "Just trying to hit the notes, ma'am."

"Nonsense." She patted his knee. "Notes are easy. Feeling is hard. You've got plenty of that."

He laughed it off, but her words hung in the air of his mind. When it was time for the last set, he walked to the microphone heavier than before. He looked out at the couples who were dancing, laughing, clinking glasses. And he thought about his empty apartment, his untouched answering machine, the guitar stand that held more dust than dreams.

He chose a song not on the list. "The Way You Look Tonight." His fingers found the chords, his voice softened, and somewhere in the middle, he stopped performing and started confessing. Each note carried the ache of missed chances, the humor of bad dates, the absurdity of crooning strangers into intimacy while his own heart idled on the sidelines.

As the last chord rang out, the hall applauded politely. But the bride clapped the loudest. Then, surprising everyone, she crossed the floor in her gown and hugged him. Whispered in his ear: "Thank you. You made it real."

Tony froze. It was just a hug. A kind word. But it cracked something open. For the first time in years, he felt seen, not as background music, not as filler, but as a man who had given a piece of himself.

Later, when the guests spilled into the night and the janitor swept away confetti, Tony lingered. He strummed one more tune, soft and private, not for the crowd but for himself. It was shaky, imperfect, but it was his. The echoes climbed the walls, and for a fleeting moment, he wasn't just a wedding singer. He was a man with a song worth singing.

He packed up his guitar, smiled at his reflection in the dark window, and whispered, "Next time, it's for me."

One Last Dance

The room was softly illuminated, and the subtle beat of the music set the tone. A layer of dust had accumulated on the faux velvet flocked walls. Bits of light from the out-of-date disco ball danced across the open space, flooding it with odd patterns on tables etched with cigarette burns.

Marie found herself by the stage, bathed in the glow of neon lights as lunchtime passed. Her joints, stiffened by arthritis, hindered her movements. Unknown to her, today's performance would be her last dance, a poignant farewell to a chapter of her life that she had outgrown. Now, she realized she had lingered in the past for too long.

Her small house, with its broken furnace and leaky roof, was on the verge of being repossessed because of her unpaid mortgage. The bills and lack of money had even pushed her to rely on friends to care for her dog. She couldn't even afford dog food.

What good was her mother's advice on finances? Her father had left them flat broke when he went off with that woman from the Dairy Queen. Marie yearned for more and felt this was her time now. She wanted money and was caught up in its allure—for a car, a trip to Hawaii, and some new clothes.

The last conversation with her mother was brief. "I'm going to make it, Mom, and I'll write every week and send money as I can. I can't do it here. You tried, and it didn't work for you, so now it's my turn." The mother's moment of foolishness was her history with a fast-talking local photographer who promised to get her revealing photos to movie studios. Now, the townspeople looked down on her as she washed dishes at the local diner, and dreams of stardom went down the drain like soapsuds.

Mentally broken by too many disappointments, Marie's mother stared at her as though she knew it might not work out. But Marie knew her mother never wanted to send her off with harsh words.

"Honey, you give it your best shot. You know I'll always be here if anything goes wrong." The tears were denied their day as she hugged Marie tightly before she watched her grab her cheap suitcase and begin walking down the front steps to the waiting car.

There had to be a solution now, years later. Something that would give her security, stability, and a sense of self-worth—feelings she had never known. If only she hadn't trusted that guy.

The man had hung around her high school's main entrance, dangling dreams of showbiz success before her eyes.

"Listen, sweetheart," he whispered as though engaged in some secretive plan, "I believe you've got potential and a great body."

The persuasion was strong. His expensive tailored suit and dazzling diamond watch added to the appeal. Why stick around for a high school diploma? What good would it do? No one in her family had one, anyway.

She danced nightly at big clubs, the promise of stardom dangling before her, not quite within reach but there, almost visible. But the better life would evaporate as the cigarette smoke, booze, and pushy strangers had. Money, something she had never had before, which came so easily, now poured out like rainwater down a spout. No thoughts about tomorrow. It was a grasshopper mentality, not one that, like the squirrel's, involved saving for the coming winter, but the rush of attention blinded her. As the bills piled up, Marie never gave them a thought.

She bought an expensive car that was later repossessed and a small home that would be in danger of being taken, too. Mortgages aren't paid with a seductive dance.

That first dance in the smoky, dark club with the eye-riveting illuminated stage was embedded in her memory. It was easy to recall the introduction that matched the horn music they played at the beginning of a corrida de toros, and then there was her new name, Candi.

Following the call of the high-pitched music, Marie pulled a matador's cape closer around her skimpy costume and swayed her body in rhythm as she mounted the stage. The cape set off her entrance with flashes of brilliance reflecting from tiny mirrors sewn into the bright red embroidered fabric.

The set hadn't come easily that day. But she knew it would become smoother; she'd learn to flirt to increase the number of bills stuffed into her costume. Such a long way from high school.

She got used to the hoots and hollers that always greeted her performances, along with the potent smell of cheap cologne and aftershaves so close it stuck to her skin. She learned to avoid grabbing hands and even the occasional drink thrown at her. No, it hadn't all been pleasant, but it was part of what she needed to do to survive.

Somewhere out in the darkness beyond her circle, where the clouds of cigarette smoke obscured the men sitting at small tables, there must be a producer, an agent, someone who would recognize her and see her talent. Where were they, and how could she get them to sign her to a film or model contract? She didn't know the questions to ask or what to expect, but she wanted fame, and fame wasn't at a strip club.

Was it the "parties" she refused or the "offers" she turned down that caused things to go wrong? Why had producers or agents missed her? No reason came to mind except that she got no help from her manager, who abandoned her for some bimbo, and off he went with Marie's money. He'd said he'd take care of her—sure.

Marie had hit a brick wall. Instead of ascending the stages of more prestigious clubs, the places were seedy now. Twenty years and no movies, no major Vegas hotels or clubs.

Gone were the men clinging and falling all over the edge of the stage, waving dollar bills as she slid across the floor or onto the pole in her sparkly outfit. A few drunk patrons now sat at this bar, hardly glancing her way.

Marie clung to the foolishness of youth even as time slipped through her fingers, not like sand but like broken glass, cutting deep within her where the scars wouldn't show. But at forty, she couldn't ignore the harsh realities of her existence. The once adoring audience whittled down to a few tired old men nursing cheap drinks, their eyes more resigned than enthralled.

She twirled around the pole, her movements a shadow of their former glory, her body protesting every bend and stretch. Even her costume, a bit of cloth and sequins, had turned against her, drooping where it should have been form-fitting. She glanced at the empty tip jar, a silent testament to her fading allure.

As she finished her set, the manager called her over. "Babe," he murmured in her ear, "your time's up. I only gave you this afternoon slot because no one else wanted it. Tomorrow, it's over. We're axing the afternoon show after that." He'd been a good guy to her, trying to help, but this was business, and he was losing money. Maybe he had his own mortgage to pay. Maybe he had his own broken dreams. Another hit to that heart in her bony chest.

But after Marie's last turn around the pole and her brief talk with the manager, her gaze caught something unexpected. In the smoky room, she noticed Sandra, her former coworker at the call center, sitting at a booth in the corner. Sandra had left half a year ago to start her virtual assistant business. The pay from that call center job has been a lifesaver, but not enough now that this job was over.

Leaning back in the worn leather booth, Sandra called out to Marie. "I've been trying to reach you. My business is growing faster than I can handle. I need someone who knows customer service and is reliable." She paused, stirring her drink. "The pay is better than this place, and you can work from home."

Marie's fingers trembled slightly as she wrapped them around a glass of water she picked up at the bar. It was an actual job, with regular hours, and no more aching joints or pitying looks. She thought of her small bungalow and how it could double as an office with a desk and a newer computer.

"I can't promise it will be easy," Sandra continued, "but I'll teach you everything I know about digital marketing and client management."

Marie nodded, feeling the familiar weight of her decisions pressing against her chest. But the weight felt different this time—like possibility rather than despair.

Afterward, she cleared out her locker for the last time. The neon lights flickered behind her as she walked out the door, her shadow stretching long and thin across the parking lot. Tomorrow, she would begin again.

The Girl

She climbs onto the local bus every Thursday morning, using both hands to pull herself up the three steps that lead to her seat at the back. Even before she gets on the bus, she has to wait and her feet are screaming because her shoes are tight on the large bunions on her feet. The driver maintains his focus on driving instead of looking at her. Most people ignore her completely. She rides the bus while holding her small shopping bag that hangs from her wrist, but now rests on her lap as she stares straight ahead at the back of the driver. No need to look at the large houses the bus is passing. No words could express how she feels—down and resigned.

The city outside the window is a dull color scheme as graffiti fades from brick surfaces and weeds emerge from sidewalk gaps while a dog investigates a trash can. The sixty-six-year-old woman sits quietly while she counts bus stops, just as she used to count stars when she was a girl.

She climbs down at the bus stop using the handrail for support while keeping her shopping bag secure with her other hand. Ten blocks to go before she reaches the house. The road lacks sidewalks, so she walks in the middle of the road while cars speed by, and the gravel beneath her feet creates a crunching sound. Her job is in the house at the end of the cul-de-sac, She keeps her body tight against the angry wind.

The house stands as a polished gem with its shutters and flowerbeds that enjoy regular mulching and tender care by the gardener. It's a display of wealth with no sign of self-awareness or loud communication.

The woman stands by the door as she does every week.

"You're late," she says, even though the time shows the woman is only two minutes past the scheduled hour.

A slight response about her arrival is attempted. The girl bends her head down. The bus took longer than usual to reach its destination this morning, but the woman turns abruptly, cutting her off in mid-sentence.

"Mm. Well, upstairs first. My friends will be here this week. The baseboards, don't forget. You missed them last time."

She speaks with an air of superiority in her voice, which sounds like a casual command for tea service. She turns her back, once again, to the woman before she can respond.

The woman, called only "my girl," sits on the floor, holding a rag filled with soapy, warm water from a small bucket. The wood surface shows gray dust particles that stick to it. She cleans the surface with care to prevent any streaks. Her knees ache. She keeps moving forward because she wants to complete her work before noon to take the noon bus back home.

A twenty-dollar bill rests on the vanity with no concealment. Not folded, not hidden. Just there.

Her breath catches. Twenty dollars would provide her with enough money to buy groceries.. The money would cover three bus fares and more. Yes, the woman pays her $15 for a half-day's work, more if she stays the day, when she'd get $20.

She stops moving with the cloth held in midair.

The woman calls from downstairs while the girl continues her work. "The furniture polish needs special attention this time because I don't want that unpleasant lemon scent to stay." It's a usual command.

The girl maintains her gaze on the bill while remaining silent.

Her mind plays the sound of her grandson's voice asking, "Grandma, can we buy cereal with marshmallows this week? The kind with the marshmallows?"

The woman calls from downstairs and wants to know what she's doing.

"Just dusting," the girl says quickly.

The bill remains there.

She reaches to grab the bill. The twenty-dollar bill appears normal, but it has an intense sense of potential. Grabbing a small dishcloth, she hurriedly crushes the bill and puts it into her pocket.

The woman quickly mounts the carpeted stairs to examine the girl's face with intense, needle-like eyes just as the girl descends from the stairs. "Did you move the vanity items? I don't want fingerprints."

"Yes, ma'am."

The woman examines her face with suspicion. "Hmm. You look flushed."

"It's warm upstairs."

"Perhaps." The woman waves her hand to show she has already forgotten about the girl. "You should finish the kitchen last. The imported crystal glasses need special care."

The girl passes by the woman; her heart continues to race.

Suddenly, the woman says today will be a full day, and she won't be leaving at noon as she thought. "I'll pay you next week. I didn't get to the bank, and you know I have to pay you in cash."

The work is finally done during the afternoon hours. The floors and mirrors reflect light, while the air carries a light scent of lavender polish. She picks up her bag as she prepares to leave.

The woman tells her to return next Thursday without looking up from her magazine reading. "Yes, ma'am."

The outside temperature has dropped. The girl takes deep breaths while her body feels both relieved and terrified.

She sits by the window on the bus ride home, holding her bag with her fingers wrapped tightly around it. She understands what her church friends would express about her actions. Taking something is theft regardless of personal need and frowned on.

The bus stops at its designated stop. A boy who appears to be sixteen years old enters while carrying a heavy backpack, which makes him slouch. He takes a seat directly across from her, displaying his restlessness by tapping his knee.

"Long day?" she asks just above a whisper.

He shrugs. "School's stupid."

She understands, and a faint smile brightens her face. The experience of school sometimes seems pointless to her. A destination waits at the end of that journey.

The boy lets out a dismissive sound before pulling his worn notebook from his backpack. A folded twenty-dollar bill slips from his pocket when he moves his body. He fails to see the money.

The girl stares at him.

The bus jumps forward in a sudden movement. The boy's backpack and the woman's shopping bag fall to the floor in a jumble of school papers, books, and things from her shopping bag. A $20 bill drifts across the floor until it rests at her feet.

She takes only a brief moment to decide before she bends down to pick it up. Her fingers wrap around the paper. She could hide the money in her bag. The boy would be unaware of it. Two twenties in one day—enough to cover groceries and bus fare for weeks.

She looks up to find his face showing the signs of hunger alongside dark circles under his eyes, which makes him seem like someone who understands what it means to be hungry. His pants bear the marks of rust from old cars and grease spots.

She extends the money to him while speaking in a soft voice. "You dropped this."

His eyes grow wide as he says, "Oh, thanks!" He takes the money, and there's a harsh tone in his voice. "I need it for our rent. The landlord told my mom, If we don't come up with some money today, he's throwing our stuff out on the street, and we'll be homeless tomorrow. This is the money the junkyard man paid me for after-school work. I pick up scraps and clean the place, and this is what I get for a week's work. My mom'll be so happy that we're not going to be homeless tomorrow."

The girl nods slightly while her throat tightens. She maintains complete silence.

She gets off the bus at her stop and struggles to keep her balance on the cracked sidewalk. The distance to her home is blocks ahead of her. She walks with purpose, unaffected by the gravel beneath her feet, as the bag remains light at her side.

Her daughter welcomes her home with a weary expression when she enters the house. "Mom, did you get your money for today?"

She removes the crumbled dishcloth from the bag before slowly unfolding it.

The twenty is gone.

Her breath catches. She does a second search of the dishcloths, the bag's seams, her skirt pockets, finding nothing.

The sudden movement of the bus must have given her bill an unexpected push, causing it to fall while she was trying to grab the money on the floor. Foolishly, she'd put her bill, wrapped in a dishcloth, in her shopping bag to keep it safe. Money was like a precious babe that needed protection from those who'd take it.

Only now does she realize she must have given the boy her twenty-dollar bill. How did that happen? There's no answer. It's gone.

Her daughter appears puzzled by her expression. "What's wrong?"

The woman stands up while attempting to hide her concern with a fake grin. "Nothing. Just tired."

She spends the night staring at the ceiling while lying in bed. Her heart experiences a strange sense of weightlessness for the very first time in a few years. The amount of money in her wallet decreased, but she discovered an unexpected value.

On Thursday, she'll board the bus as she carries her shopping bag the way she does every Thursday. The woman will continue to address her as "the girl," but this time she won't experience any feeling of shame from the word.

She understands a truth that the woman wouldn't understand about giving without expecting anything in return when you possess almost no resources.

Between the Lines

Seth Martin readjusted his headset for the hundredth time during the day while the camera operators prepared for their next taping session. At twenty-two years old, Seth achieved his career goal when he became a production assistant at Channel 15 News. The demanding nature of his work didn't concern him because he enjoyed being part of the team that delivered nightly news broadcasts to home audiences.

The production assistant, Martin, shouted his assignment. He had to pick up coffee for Derek, who served as the lead producer. Seth nodded before taking his car keys. The coffee delivery proved to be the most unpleasant part of his day at work, although every employee needed to begin their career with demeaning, low-level responsibilities. And he was at the bottom of the career ladder. No sense complaining; that was just the way it was.

The production team gathered at Tommy Davis's apartment to celebrate their successful ratings for that week. Seth spent his evening at Tommy Davis's apartment drinking beer and feeling uncomfortable because of the senior staff members there. The workplace environment didn't suit him and he stayed quiet while performing his duties effectively, yet never felt acceptance by his colleagues.

The room fell silent when Derek spoke, his words cutting through the music. "The coffee boy, who usually only delivered drinks, now drinks beer," according to Derek.

The entire room burst into laughter at that moment. Seth attempted to smile, but his face turned red with embarrassment. "Yeah, well, sometimes."

Derek continued his teasing by asking Seth if he had ever experienced any wild moments in his life. "Have you ever tried marijuana, or do you stick to school rules about bedtime?"

More laughter. Seth's fingers tightened until his knuckles turned white as he pressed against his beer glass. "I've done stuff."

"Like what? Did you ever break the rule of getting home after ten at night?"

The public humiliation was searing, so intense that it created waves of embarrassment throughout his body. He was the center of attention in the room, where most of them leaned against the furniture, staring at him as they waited for his answer. Famous for his outrageous tales, the cameraman Marcus stepped forward on Seth's behalf. "Now, this is going to make your world super again."

Marcus led Seth to a hidden area where he revealed his plan to show him something extraordinary. "This experience isn't suitable for beginners."

Seth should have left the situation immediately. He should have gone back home to Queens, where he could watch TV before going to bed early. The drive with Marcus to his place took only twenty minutes. As Seth watched, the guy prepared something he had only seen in movies. Then it was time for the adventure.

The needle entered his skin with less resistance than he had anticipated. And then—

The world transformed. All his concerns, together with his feelings of shame and self-doubt, disappeared completely as the summer sun melted the winter snow. A sensation of warm honey enveloped him while he drifted through air that felt like pure happiness. Seth experienced his first moment of absolute perfection during that instant.

"Holy shit," he whispered.

Marcus grinned. "The good life has welcomed you to its world, young man."

Seth kept his work schedule for three months after his initial experiment. He maintained his professional conduct at work by avoiding drug use. The time between noon and one o'clock, however, became his most important daily block of time. He would drive to the studio's nearby rough neighborhood to meet Marcus or his friends for his daily escape.

But his mother was a bit more observant than he realized. "Your face looks tired to me, mijo," as he ate his breakfast. "You're not eating enough food? Maybe at work you skip lunch?"

"I'm okay, Ma. Just working hard." Seth kept his head down while he ate his cereal, not noticing its taste.

His father looked up from reading his newspaper. "You should take a break because you've been working too much." They had no idea about his situation.

The habit of using had progressed from its initial fling into something more. It cost him more than his salary as an assistant. Desperation forced him to find some way to get money. It could be in the apartment buildings near the studio.

It started simply. The unlocked residents' doors during daytime hours made it easy for him to enter and exit buildings during his lunch break. He assured himself that he was not a thief. He considered his actions to be temporary property loans to survive. Yeah, these were just loans. He'd repay them in time. Just loans.

Credit cards were the easiest. The dealer took credit cards as payment for drugs because people didn't report their missing cards until two days had passed. Seth developed a method to enter and exit buildings within five minutes, using only one card from each residence and avoiding a repetition of visits to the same building. Snake, the dealer, was overjoyed by Seth's progress. During an afternoon meeting, he tossed off a casual comment: "You're getting good at this. Natural talent."

The remark made Seth's stomach feel queasy instead of proud. He felt sick. And the absence of heroin made him feel worse than his current feeling of being sick.

Trying to continue hiding his injection spots, he noticed a tiny red spot between his toes. It was the first sign of his problem. Seth made sure to inject his heroin in areas that remained hidden from view by using the spaces between his toes, which remained concealed under his socks and shoes. The red spot grew into a more painful, inflamed area. It didn't matter where he shot up, the red spot was expanding, and it was so painful.

He examined his foot in his childhood bedroom while muttering, "Shit" because the infection spread from his toes to his ankle through red lines. The swelling of his toe made it extremely hot to the touch while the infection spread upward like an ugly branch to his ankle.

Even walking during his shift was difficult. A slight limp was developing and became noticeable by the crew. Every movement of his foot created intense burning sensations.

Beth from the video department asked if everything was okay because he appeared to be in terrible condition. "You look like hell."

Seth pretended to be exhausted while he used his desk for support to maintain his balance.

The pain in his foot became so severe that he needed to use both hands for support when he tried to walk. By Thursday of that week, it was increasingly clear that he could not go on like this. The infection was spreading, Today, he had to deliver payments to Snake because it was his regular visit.

The apartment building located on Fifth Street was Seth's regular Thursday destination. Third floor, apartment 3B. The elderly woman who lived there always left her door unlocked and kept her purse on the kitchen counter. Easy money.

A cool October air brought a few brief moments of relief from sweat as he climbed the stairs. His eyes became hazy as he attempted to turn the door handle.

The door was locked.

He repeated the attempt to open the door while whispering, "No, no, no," to himself. The card remained his only hope because Snake wouldn't delay, and Seth's body was starting to experience withdrawal symptoms.

Panic overtook judgment. Seth repeatedly pushed his shoulder against the door until either the doorframe or his shoulder broke without him being able to determine which one.

He stepped into the apartment before stopping dead in his tracks.

Mrs. Rodriguez stood in her kitchen with a teacup while watching Seth with a sense of sadness instead of fear.

"You finally returned to my place as I had expected," she whispered. "I've been keeping track. My credit card, then my grandson's. You work at the TV station as the young man who operates cameras, right?"

Seth's knees failed him. He dropped to the linoleum floor of her kitchen while his body convulsed. "I'm sorry. I'm so sorry. I don't understand what happened because I never wanted this to happen."

"Look at your foot, mijo."

Seth followed her direction to see blood dripping from his sock into his shoe.

The next sentence she uttered caused him to shiver even more. "You're dying, young man." She set down her tea before grabbing her phone to call emergency services.

"No, please. I'll lose my job. My parents—"

"Your parents show their love for you through their actions. Your death would turn all your employment history into something meaningless. You can always get another job, but you can't get another life."

Attempting to rise from the floor, he found his injured leg had completely failed him. A searing hot poker was wedged between his toes, and he felt himself falling off an emotional cliff. The infection had spread beyond what he had initially thought. His entire body burned with intense heat.

A cool towel on his forehead seemed to help a bit while he asked her why she had chosen to help him.

She explained she had a grandson his age and that Seth was someone's child who was both frightened and unwell. Mrs. Rodriguez knew the drill.

The approaching sirens grew louder. It was a sound he both welcomed and feared.

"What about my parents? They don't know. They think I'm working hard at my job."

"They'll uncover the truth about you." Mrs. Rodriguez was reassuring, even though she didn't know how his parents would react, but he needed this now. "Your parents might find your death easier to accept than losing their child like this, but your parents may surprise you."

The paramedics pushed their way into the apartment through the broken door as Seth shut his eyes. As though he were a small child, they lifted him up, put him on a collapsible gurney, and quickly carried him out of the apartment. All the while, Mrs. Rodriguez watched from her window with a sad expression instead of anger as she held her teacup. She wasn't angry at Seth, but at the people who had done this to him.

Seth turned off his phone after his thumb strayed near the keyboard. They'd know soon enough.

The ambulance driver slammed the gas pedal down, throwing everything inside backwards for a brief few seconds as they sped ahead toward the hospital. His departure was reflected in the window, which showed him as a pale face with red eyes and a person who looked nothing like him. The transition from his first perfect high to this present moment had erased his true self from existence. All he was now was a walking shadow and a willing victim for his dealer.

He believed there was still time to discover his path back to himself. But making it back wouldn't be easy, and he didn't know who would help. There must be someone, he was thinking, someone out there who will help, but how will I find them?

The red marks on his leg throbbed with each heartbeat, serving as a warning about his near-death experience. Slowly, everything seemed to fade and go quiet as the ambulance screamed through the night toward the emergency room. But Seth would lie quietly and wait for his savior.

Moment of Truth

S unlit days bring no joy for Jeffrey, who hurriedly and carefully closes his scuffed shoes with the thinning laces. The apartment was cold last night, and he wanted to dress quickly. Then he looks down at his shoes once again.

His mother has expressed some relief that his feet don't seem to grow like other children; she'd have to buy new shoes if they did. Now, he stands up unsteadily on the shoes whose soles work like rocker rungs from too many half-soled repairs that save the money whole soles would cost. Another day lies ahead of him.

The morning in class is uneventful. Jeffrey has been called to the board once to diagram a sentence, and he does it well. But he knows something awaits him in the school lunchroom.

After class, he heads down the green corridor to the old iron staircase, occasionally slipping on his rocker shoes. He begins to feel a change in his heartbeat and a steady rise in temple pain.

Once in the smelly, overheated lunchroom, Jeffrey lingers at the tail end of the line, his empty tray a conspicuous plea. His eyes widen in anticipation. Softly, he urges his classmates to pass ahead, his unspoken wish woven into the tapestry of these shared moments.

As the last students receive their meals, Jeffrey approaches the steam table. The absence of a lunch ticket is making the air thick with uncertainty. Having pushed the tray toward the two women manning the steam table, he jingles three nickels in his pocket. Yeah, he returned deposit bottles, but it's not enough—he knows it.

Behind the counter, the white-uniformed women engage in an intense exchange, their faces revealing a nuanced dance between compassion and financial burden.

One woman, her features softened by empathy, motions to give the boy a free lunch. Her eyes, like windows into a generous soul, softened with smile wrinkles. Standing firm, the other, a stern figure marked by the weight of personal struggles, insists on payment.

The women's voices, now a less-than-delicate symphony of discord, rise above the ambient student chatter. Her face is an effortful display of frustration, and the first woman brings forth a poignant reminder—a past act of kindness, a loan given in a moment of shared humanity. Loud voices rise like a human vapor behind the steam table.

"If I hadn't given you that gas money, would you be at work today or wondering if you'd have a job tomorrow? How many lottery tickets did you buy, anyway?" The question lingers in the air, casting shadows on the delicate facial balances of compassion and self-preservation.

Jeffrey, a passive observer turned unwitting participant, stands at the epicenter of this human drama. The lunchroom, once alive with the hum of youthful banter, stops, as though a heavy curtain has fallen, into an uneasy silence as students turn to watch.

Amidst the tense tableau, a resolution unfolds. The second woman, her heart softened by the weight of memories and a selfish need for future acts of kindness, nods in reluctant acknowledgment. A gesture, a silent agreement, and the boy moves forward, his tray now a vessel for shared sustenance without a lunch ticket.

Seated at a table, he exchanges a fleeting but knowing glance at the woman who had championed his cause. The lunchroom, once fractured, gradually returns to the shared experience of lunchtime, restoring a sense of unity.

But tomorrow will bring another trip to the lunchroom, perhaps with a few more nickels in Jeffrey's pocket. Today, after school, he has to scour the neighborhood for the all-important beer return bottles that garner a nickel each. Two more bottles, and he'll pay for lunch. He knows where to look along the highway.

Legacy of Letters

T he small packet creates a burning sensation in my jacket pocket while I cycle through deserted streets. Mrs. Henderson revealed the location to me during one of those sleepy Wednesday sessions when she spoke softly while the timekeeper kept running its scheduled rhythm. She took my hand with her thin fingers which seemed almost transparent while saying, "The pink peonies contain the truth when I am gone. Look there."

I believed she experienced sundowning according to Mom's explanation of how elderly people sometimes behave. She presented me with a photograph showing three women wearing hairnets and lipstick while standing in front of a B-17 bomber. She stood in the center of the photograph while her arms wrapped around the other two women. The back of the photograph displayed faded ink writing which read, "Betty, Rose, & me—the things we did for love and country."

The three letters rested on my bedroom desk. The yellow ribbon on the package made my hands shake while I untied it. Despite its delicate appearance, like a moth wing, the handwriting was exact, and urgent. In 1944, the letters came from London using a no longer existing address.

The first message starts with "Dearest Rose. We cannot reverse the actions we have already performed. The information exists at the location we previously established." The message continues with "If you are reading this, then I am already..."

The text message from Mrs. Henderson's nephew arrives on my phone while I'm reading her letters. He knows. His following message brought me a surprise when he typed:

"She left something for you. A box in her closet. Visit tomorrow before the estate sale to collect the item she left for you."

The entire night became a sleepless period. The letters describe three female codebreakers who worked with classified intelligence to save thousands of lives through their betrayal, which led to the execution of one man. Three generations of family members suffered from the decision Mary and her friends made during 1944.

But something is missing. The last part of the letter stops abruptly in the middle of a sentence as if...

The box. Of course.

I returned to her house the following day. The nephew provided entry while showing no interest as he pointed toward the flight of stairs. He walked me to the upstairs room after stating that she discussed me with him. "She said you reminded her of Rose."

The box contains a small amount of dust and has a brown paper covering with a thin yellow ribbon securing it. The package has a thin sheet of paper and a rusty key, which I discovered inside.

The final letter contains a different date than 1944. Mrs. Henderson wrote the letter in her unsteady hand during the previous month.

"Sarah you remain the last person who understands the truth. The revelation of truth does not always bring liberation because it can transfer the burden of concealed secrets from one generation to the next. The safe deposit box can be accessed by using this key. The decision about what to do with the contents rests with you. Certain secrets need to stay hidden but others require exposure to daylight. You will recognize it when you see it.

Love,

Mary (who was never really a Henderson)."

I placed the musty box back together while her trust enveloped me in an unnoticeable shroud. The nephew watches me with a suspicious expression. "She told me you would figure out what to do," according to him.

I held the box against my body like a delicate child that someone had given me to protect. The sun shines brightly outside while people remain unaware that their historical records face either permanent concealment or complete revelation. The decision together with the key now rests in my hands.

I opened the box during the night when darkness spread across my bedroom walls. The three women appear in the same photograph but now they face a park instead of a bomber. The women stand before a park while their faces show deep concern. The back of the photograph shows fifteen names written by different hands. I identify all fifteen individuals who are now prominent figures, including senators and scientists and military leaders.

Their lives would be ruined if these secrets were revealed. The list of coordinates appears below the names, which I found by searching on Google. The coordinates direct me to a cemetery where I discover the unmarked burial site of the man whose death resulted from their collective silence.

The letters reveal that the man who died was actually a hero who gave his all to protect their secret operations. I light a match to watch the letters transform into blackened ash as they burn away in my kitchen sink. The photograph I will preserve serves as proof of three women who bore the burden of decisions that seemed beyond human reach. Certain truths remain too expensive to reveal during our present time. The most compassionate version of history emerges when we choose to conceal certain facts.

I hide the key beneath Mrs. Henderson's peony flowers, which share the same pale color as her valueless print. Future generations will discover the key after all names in the photograph have disappeared from memory. I will safeguard the silence that defends the people who never wanted to bear the burden of their ancestors' conflict.

Some Must Pay

T he roads are nothing more than wrong strips of mud separating two long lines of house after house after house of the same design, with few exceptions. Here and there is a small, no basement, ranch house for those who are't looking to expand their family or who have limited income. The streetlights are still not installed, except for one or two placed down the long strip that extends to a seeming horizon, the main highway.

When it rains, the muddy roads are a slushy mess that presents considerable walking difficulties. There are no sidewalks, and there will be no sidewalks. Sidewalks encourage interlopers to enter into these tight-knit neighborhoods of families fresh from the city, seeking a better life. The young women are left at home to care for the children while their husbands go off to menial jobs on the railroad or new construction in the area. They're alone and vulnerable, and it's a formula perfect for the hawks who come to pick at whatever is available. These little sparrows are sitting there waiting.

Leads for the salesmen are easily gotten by slipping a $20 bill to the man at the utilities company who hooks up the new meters once the young families move into just-built homes. Once the lead is in hand, the machinery goes into high gear as the salesman practices his pitch, full of ways to increase sales by any means possible.

He plans to adopt an approach that incorporates the mother's desire to assist her children in learning to read, the role of religion in the household, and the fact that certain needs can't be accommodated in a budget. This goes beyond mere budgeting; it addresses the fundamental needs of the children. Hopefully, he knows this will be the approach that will get her to sign the contract to keep the books coming monthly along with those monthly invoices. After all, his manager is pushing for increased sales, and he knows he needs to pay his bills.

The salesman approaches 47 Maple Street with his professional smile in place. A woman with a baby on her hip steps out to answer the door while her two older children pull her cheap housedress around her legs and peek out.

The salesman presents himself as someone wanting to discuss educational opportunities for her children. Certainly, she has two who need to learn to read and another who will need that skill shortly.

She recognizes him as the encyclopedia man Mrs. Cary warned her about. It was the first call from her new neighbor, and it was a concern that she had fresh in her mind.

He tells her that he got his contact information from the utility company and slipped in a word about his need to earn a living like her husband. Uncomfortable for a moment, she slips the baby to her other hip.

"I know all about the need to read and to have excellent reading abilities because I used to work as a teacher aid before World War II."

His smile disappears from his face. The situation is not following his planned sequence.

He lets his body droop downward. His commission is vanishing before his eyes.

"How about a cup of coffee and a pot roast sandwich? I just made a pot, and there's plenty of roast. My mother-in-law came to visit last night, so there was extra."

He spends twenty minutes at her kitchen table sharing his daughter's illness story while she treats him like family by feeding him. The coffee and the sandwich loosen him up enough to tell her that the school district offered him part-time maintenance work, which would be a better opportunity than his failed sales attempt. Not only would he have a steady salary but also health insurance.

Sometimes, the actual treasure we seek exists beyond our initial search targets. Yup, he was going into maintenance work.

The Big Break

Alarm clocks make noise that penetrates thin walls, and if you want to filch your neighbor's copy of a weekly trade publication, an alarm clock is the last thing you want sounding off in your room.

The clever act of swiftly snatching and quickly scanning the columns of ads for actors had become a skill in which he was a perfectionist. You had to be, or you wouldn't make it in this business. Making it was all he had ever dreamed of since he was a little boy in elementary school.

It was the trade ad he had been waiting for. Eyes widening, he tried to slow his heart, but it was no use. Blood was rushing through his body, and sweat glowing on his forehead.

In bold type, it read, "TV food commercial shoot, male/female actors, male 20s-30s, older woman, ethnic Italian family types."

It's all he wanted, and he fit the part. He had spent years meticulously working as a statistical typist in all those temp jobs. Now was his chance, and he was going to make a TV commercial if it killed him.

He knows the part is right for him, and he needs the money. His landlord's latest notice had a tone that was easily understood. But more than that, he needs the exposure this commercial provides an actor. It's his chance to break through, to make it.

Enough sitting in those dark, smelly hallways waiting for a call into dimly lit old rehearsal rooms to be faced by a few guys just over their pimple-popping age who barely lift their heads and look at him like he's groceries. The remarks sound like they're looking at sides of beef, and they check him off on their clipboards as they do grocery items in a store.

The cell phone rings with an irritating jangling noise like broken glass. He needs to answer the call. It's from his agent, Harry. An audition opportunity has appeared after his relentless daily calls.

"Hello, Harry? Yeah, yeah, I know you're doing me a favor because of my brother, but this won't be like any of the other times. I promise, I'll do better this time. I'll get this gig. It's perfect for me."

The cell shakes from the tremor of his hand, and his sweat greases it as if it is trying to escape. Even the phone wants to be away from him.

Why won't they let him forget the pills were an accident? It wasn't his intention to overdose. He's OK now, but they still won't let him forget it.

With a brief phone conversation and a request to arrive at work slightly later, he stands a chance to get the gig. The room's above a betting parlor near a strip joint and it's empty, except for the infamous table and three men. His success is in question; he feels like he's facing a firing squad.

"Yeah, hair is okay, skin not too dark. Straight teeth. Not too tall but thin enough." In a sotto voce tone, the guy asks the other two, "But don't you think he's too old? He's got to be over thirty."

"Shhhh, he'll do for now," one barely whispers out of the side of his mouth.

"Thin, so people want Momma to feed him, right?" Another snickers in less-than-a-stage whisper. It's loud enough to unnerve Eddie.

They don't offer him a chair. He's forced to stand before them as they roll their eyes up and down his body and his clothing.

"He doesn't smell, does he?" one asks the other two—the three laugh with no regard for him. It's as though he doesn't exist in this room.

"Okay, read this." He pushes a sheet of paper with three lines toward the edge of the table, causing it to almost flutter to the floor. The text is difficult to read, but Eddie manages to read it aloud in one attempt.

"Okay, that's all right, and you look like what we need; you've got that darkish complexion and that black hair. But we need more than you," the half-turned-around youngest with the toothpick in his mouth utters almost into the air.

"We need more of your ethnic types. You know, your relative types and a momma, too. You got relatives? Yeah, we need relatives. Is that something you can do, kid?"

The "kid" comment smacked his ears like a sock with a roll of coins in it. Relatives? Did he have relatives? What was this anyway?

"And not just any relatives. You know, we need cousins and uncles, and they need to be dressed as though they're hanging around the house waiting for Momma to make dinner. Nothing fancy, you know, just plain clothes. The momma type has to be special, too. Got it, kid? Not just any momma type, but one you'd see hanging out a window yelling for the kids to come in for supper. Got it, kid? She has to be like an older Sophia Loren, with the same sexiness. Get the picture, kid?" The description continued for another two minutes.

If the momma type were described in greater detail, he'd need a pad to write it all down. The guy wanted something he didn't have, but he'd learned years ago from an acting coach that you always tell them you have what they want, even if you don't.

The older momma-type had to meet the requirements that the toothpick-chewing, just-out-of-college guy—or was he just out of high school?—was outlining as though he were speaking to a moron.

She had to have gray hair, "but not too gray," and be slightly overweight "but charming and with a good, hearty, but sexy laugh." And then he added, "You know, like the momma you want to take back to the apartment, get it?" The wink cinched it. It sounded like he was describing a dish on a plate in a restaurant. He was food, and these guys were the meatgrinders.

Back at the office, he rounded up the leftover evening staff around the coffee wagon and selected types he could use for his ruse. To each, he cautiously whispered an invitation. They loved it! Commercials? All of them were eager and trooped over to the rehearsal hall with Eddie a few evenings later. There were no hitches, and they loved his "momma," who resembled an older, attractive version of Loren. The pimply one was impressed.

"Okay, there are no lines, so all you have to do is stand around the way we place you, and Momma has to yell for you to come in. All you need to do is yell. Momma, let me hear you yell."

Inhaling deeply and almost popping a button on her blouse in the process, "Momma" let out a scream that made them all jump. Who knew she could yell like that?

"Yeah," she chirped, "I used to call the rest of the family to dinner because my momma was too busy, so I had lots of practice. Haven't used that in years."

The cattle call was over; they disappeared into the night until the next evening when he'd see them at work again.

In the office, in an area off to the side where he wouldn't be heard, he stared at the lump of black plastic before him. Devoid of any humanity, its electronic circuits and plain numbered buttons told unwanted tales. The memories and turn-downs felt flung in his face by the unit.

Forcing himself to push his hand forward, he picked up the receiver, punched in the numbers slowly, and waited. It was the waiting that never seemed to end. Now it was even longer.

Today, the office evening staff was chatting about something that brought brief waves of laughter to fill the empty space. What could it be?

He listened, but all he heard was, "Yeah, today, this morning." And then the other sentences came tumbling out, and he got that knot in his stomach.

"Yes, she called in today and told her boss that he could take the job and shove it. Can you believe she'd use language like that? She's always presented herself as though she's European royalty and we're simply American riffraff. Yeah, that slight accent helped. Was it real, do you think?"

Laughter is louder now with nodding of heads and hands held to mouths to suppress laughs too much for an office.

A cheery voice responded to his call. "Oh, yeah, Eddie. The reading was perfect; everyone worked great, especially your friend. They made the choice, and the woman you found to play your mother was signed for the commercial."

He held himself back and murmured, "You mean," he replied haltingly, "I didn't get a role, but she did?"

The "momma" woman, a file clerk, had never acted in her life, had money from her husband's estate, and hadn't wanted to go to the audition. He had to plead with her to accompany him. They wanted ethnic types, and one was needed for the momma part.

He'd promised to input data for her, take her out to dinner, and do anything she wanted if she came with him. For God's sake, he'd even sleep with her if she'd agreed to this one favor. Well, maybe that wouldn't have been a favor only for her. She was a little Loren-ish.

The commercial ran for three months, and the checks rolled into her bank account. Now, she had representation and appeared in advertisements when a sultry, ethnic maternal figure was desired. She seamlessly adapted to this new lifestyle. Her only competition had died months ago, and she was the sole choice for the roles. Bad enough that she had gotten the role, but he had to pass an enormous billboard with her on it, showing her using a bank ATM. Each time he looked at it, it was another blow to his ego.

Enough with the rejections, he was thinking. He was tired of being told he was too short, too thin, that his hair wasn't right, that he was getting older, and that he had a Queens accent.

Twelve floors up, the expansive glass window looked back at him, blank as always, but now with a special message. He understood.

Personal Shopper

The doors are unlocked by neatly dressed men leaning down to push keys into the floor locks. Almost before they're standing upright, women with shopping bags are energetically, shoulder first, pushing through the doors in their frantic attempt to get at sale merchandise before anyone else can beat them to it. It's a rush that happens every sale day, and everyone knows the crowds will be restless, the women will be short-tempered, and the saleswomen will be swamped. They all know what is expected, especially Mary, who depends on the unruly crowds, the hassles, and the distraction that will afford her free access to what she has come for, not to purchase, but to obtain.

Dressed in an oversized and drab raincoat, with a scarf, or rather a kerchief, tied around her head and pulled close to her face, she is alert to any of the store detectives who may mix with the crowd in their attempts to stop shoplifting, her specialty.

Mary had been working the department stores for years now, ever since her neighbor Mrs. Simons had mentioned needing a nice dress for her daughter's wedding but couldn't afford the prices. "You're so clever, Mary," she'd said. "I bet you could figure something out." And Mary had.

The system was perfect. Five dresses into the fitting room, three on under her coat, and she walks out calm as you please. If caught—which happened maybe one time in ten—she'd mention her condition. Mary has a psychiatric history and has been hospitalized numerous times. She uses that as a "get out of jail free" card whenever possible. When caught, she would watch the security guards' faces change from anger to discomfort. They'd take back the merchandise and escort her to the door themselves, just to get rid of the problem.

But today, something felt different. The young security guard, who'd been watching her, wasn't backing down like the others.

"Ma'am, I understand you have challenges," he said in a hushed tone, "but I also know you've been in here four times this month. My name is David, and I think maybe we can help each other out."

Mary's heart raced. This wasn't how it usually went. "I told them I have a mental condition, I'm a psychiatric patient. I get confused sometimes." Mary knew very well she wasn't confused at all. As a matter of fact, she knew exactly what she was doing. She knew which department to go to, where to find the exact sizes that she needed, and which dressing rooms had the fewest employees in the area. It was all a well-planned scheme, and all she had to do was remember the sizes and the styles. Mary carried no notes with her so that if she were stopped, there would be no evidence against her. Yes, Mary was clever.

David smiled. "My sister has schizophrenia, too. And you know what? She's the smartest person I know. Just like you're smart enough to coordinate sizes, remember what people want, and run what's basically a personal shopping service."

Mary stared at him. No one had ever called what she did a business before.

"Look," David continued, "my manager's been complaining that we need help during sale days. Someone who understands what customers really want, someone who can spot trouble before it starts. Someone who knows this store inside and out." He paused. "The pay isn't great, but it's honest. And there's a discount for employees."

Six months later, Mary was the best personal shopper the store had ever hired. She had a knack for knowing exactly what would look good on a customer, could spot a shoplifter from across the floor, and had turned her neighborhood operation into legitimate referrals that earned her commissions. In fact, Mary was so good that she could spot people who used "crotching" to put small appliances between their thighs and walk right out of the store without anybody ever suspecting them of stealing. How did she learn that skill? Yes, she used to do that a few times, but then she decided it was much easier to get the dresses.

Mrs. Simons got her wedding dress with Mary's employee discount. And every morning Mary came to work, in her own clothes now, no more oversized raincoat. David would wave from the security office and call out, "How's business, partner?"

These days she could tell her boyfriend Al, the local gravedigger, how well she was doing and that she was getting commissions and didn't have to worry about the police anymore. Mary would smile and think about how sometimes the best endings were the ones you never saw coming.

Breaking Glass

Madison held the champagne bottle tightly in her hand. The string of lights she had installed that morning trimmed the crystal-clear water of her family's infinity pool in front of her. It was just what she wanted, and it created shimmering starlight effects. The hired band finished their third set while thirty of her closest friends, whom she couldn't recall by name, cheered behind her. The event followed a standard pattern, yet it lacked the feeling of being ordinary. Yeah, Madison knew how to throw a party.

Jake shouted at her to throw the bottle while claiming her parents would never know the truth. The smashed glass in the pool would create a hilarious situation when everyone returned home. Although it was juvenile, nobody recognized that at the time.

She had become accustomed to the deception. Her parents believed she spent her time studying for good grades while helping animals at the local shelter. The grade slips she forged, her hidden stash, and her grandmother's jewelry sales became her source of funding for these parties. Besides, her parents were away for a while, and she had the house all to herself.

Madison raised the bottle high into the air. The Moët & Chandon bottle glittered in the moonlight. This one bottle exceeded the weekly earnings of most people. She took the bottle from her father's wine cellar without thinking, just as she did with everything else.

The crowd started chanting for her to break the bottle. They formed a slow-moving wave that resembled a stadium event while standing and sitting down, but they were in her parents' swimming pool area. The pool house started moving in time with the crowd as people pushed against it.

She threw the bottle. A glinting dark arc, speeding toward the edge of the pool, pulled their eyes upward. With all her strength, she flung it. It crashed into the pool's marble edge, creating a loud explosion that sent dark shards flying into the water like festive confetti. The crowd roared.

"More! More!"

Chloe brought two bottles of vintage Chateau Margaux Bordeaux to Madison, almost tripping over her sandals because of her intoxication. She laughed while showing the bottles to Madison because they had simply been left unattended. "The purpose of money is to enable people to have enjoyable times," she slurred.

The two friends stood together with their bottles, waiting to strike the pool edge. Breaking glass, joyful sounds, and musical notes filled the air around them. Partygoers started grabbing bottles from the outdoor bar, the wine cellar, and any other location they could find. The pool was now transformed into a sparkling mess of red wine and champagne bubbles, which rose from the bottom as glass fragments and corks floated on the surface.

The feeling of power and invincibility washed over Madison as she stood there. The house was hers, and so were the pool and this act of defiance. The act of destruction brought her a sense of importance that her parents could never buy with their wealth.

The party continued until the first light of dawn appeared. After everyone left the party or collapsed on the leather couches, the pool transformed into a crime scene. Thousands of dollars' worth of alcohol sank into contaminated water in the pool. It was an ugly mess, lurking like a horrible monster, ready to injure anyone who foolishly approached it.

Madison stood alone on the patio, still intoxicated, as she looked at the destruction she had caused. The house was unoccupied. Her parents wouldn't return for three days. She had enough time to come up with a clever solution. She always did. This time it might be a bit more difficult. It wasn't only that expensive wine, but also the pool that was an enormous shard of broken glass. Could she find someone to assist in fixing that?

She entered the house to grab her phone to call the pool maintenance service but stopped dead in her tracks; her parents were sitting at the kitchen island.

Her mother gazed at Madison with eyes that Madison had never seen before. They showed no anger or disappointment but complete emptiness. Hollow, like her very soul had been pulled out of her, Madison knew that moment would come one day.

Her father began explaining why the sudden return of her parents was significant. He pulled up a video on his phone; it showed her throwing bottles into the pool while glass shattered all around her.

"The neighbors contacted us at midnight. They expressed their concern about your safety. With all the noise and the smashing glass, they figured there must be a problem."

Madison expected her parents to start yelling, but instead they stared at her with faces that seemed completely unfamiliar. Her father's face was ashen, his mouth half-open, as though in shock.

"Why?" her father asked. The sound of his voice had that quality that you only hear in wounded animals. Yes, he was a wounded animal tonight.

Madison began to speak, but her words felt meaningless as she tried to explain her situation. "You spend all your time away from home and show no interest in anything that matters to me." Now it was a child's voice that was crying out in this empty mansion bought with precious hours stolen from their child.

Her mother's voice broke as she asked, "We don't care?" Of course, the mother never thought that all the parties she had to throw and the events she had to go to when it should have been bedtime story time weren't significant. Neither parent could claim a lack of guilt. But in desperation, they tried.

"Madison, we were working nonstop for sixteen hours to fund your grandmother's cancer treatment. The wine you broke was meant for a sale to fund your grandmother's medical expenses. We stopped being super rich when your father's careless investments caused us to lose most of our money. We thought we could pretend to be rich and go on with life, so we didn't tell you."

The room started to rotate around her. Madison held onto the counter for support. "What, are you serious? Grandma is perfectly healthy. She sent me a postcard from Europe during the previous month."

Her parents shared a new expression, which she had never witnessed before.

"Your mother never told you the fact that Grandma was in hospice care for three months. The postcards we sent to you were actually sent by friends for us because we wanted to help you avoid your senior year stress."

The hospital became their permanent residence during all of their business trips. They weren't business trips at all, but brief visits with her grandmother.

The school had reached out to her parents about the frequent absences during the previous months. Her father's office had been sending all her school communications to her parents since the beginning. "Your friend at the office told us about all of your school activities, including drinking and partying. We chose to remain silent because we wanted you to seek help." Her mother's voice was low, almost devoid of emotion, as she looked down at the floor and her hands that were constantly rubbing together.

The pool area displayed a sad scene of broken glass and waste, which mirrored the sun's rays like shattered dreams. Madison believed her parents were uninterested in her life, but she actually harmed the people who protected her from the truth. At least they believed they were shielding her from the truth, thinking it was beneficial to prevent any interference with her schoolwork.

The party guests started sending her messages through her phone, but she turned it off.

"How much time does she have?" Her mother whispered that her life expectancy was between five and seven days.

Madison nodded while her tears ran in steady, transparent streams down her cheeks. She studied her parents with new attention for the first time. When did his hair turn completely gray? When did the lines that formed around her mother's eyes become visible, and at what time?

She asked to visit her grandmother. "Can we visit her?"

The three of them shared their first homecoming in months when her parents agreed to visit her grandmother together. Maybe it would be a new beginning, and they certainly hoped that would be the out-come of this sad event. But no one knew.

Secret Sauce

Richard Mallory faced more issues than any amount of bourbon drinking or YouTube tutorials could solve. His girlfriend Simone told him he was "emotionally unavailable," which made him feel like a bank machine with an "Out of Service" notice attached to it. Using the word "redundant," the advertising firm's manager suggested Richard's position was unnecessary, causing him to imagine himself out on the street with no job. Great.

On his way home that evening, the discovery of a pop-up tent on a side street between a tarot card reader and a sock vendor brought him unexpected rescue.

A handwritten sign on the folding table shouted "Secret Sauce" in bold letters. A thin vendor with a clown-like smile, who appeared to be using rented equipment, leaned toward him from behind the display.

"Try it?" the vendor asked.

Richard twirled the plastic squeeze bottles in his hand. The "troops" were arranged in military formation. He maintained his skepticism. "*What's in it*?"

The man replied with: "Flavor! and maybe even something else." It cost one dollar.

The price was affordable. Why not? Richard paid for the small bottle, pushed it into his deep coat pocket, and completely forgot about it until later in the evening while deciding on dinner. The challenges were in his fridge. Expired eggs, wilted spinach, and frozen pizza faced him. No, not anything he wanted. The pizza was tossed into the microwave before adding the sauce as a last-minute addition. Why not? If he bought the sauce for flavor, this was where he'd use it.

The moment the sauce touched his tongue, Richard stopped moving. Staring down at the slice, he found nothing unusual, but the flavor, the flavor was incredible and he wanted more. He couldn't resist it.

The wood-fired dough transformed into a perfect blistered crust, while the rubbery cheese was now an authentic Italian mozzarella. He felt transported to a Roman dinner setting, where he sat under candlelight while a sommelier brought him an additional glass of Chianti.

Richard whispered, "Holy hell," while he licked his fingers. Each bit of sauce sent waves of pleasure down his body, and, for once in a long time, he felt content. He was like a child discovering something wonderful and exciting. The sauce? It was only the sauce?

A single drop on two scrambled eggs transformed his breakfast into a Ritz-Carlton Hotel experience. Coffee with a splash? He was transported into a Parisian café experience. Gazing out his window at Mrs. Kravitz watering her geraniums, he surprisingly waved at her. She returned the gesture. Usual? No, not usual. He'd never given her so much as a quick smile in all the time he'd lived in his apartment.

And it didn't stop. Richard started greeting his long-forgotten neighbors throughout the entire week. The postman. The dog walker. The teenager who performed his skateboard tricks during early morning hours received a greeting from him. Simone saw his transformation during their following dinner together. She never noticed him adding two drops to the soy sauce. Ok, he was being sneaky, but so what if it made things so much better?

Richard smiled while the soy sauce mixed with Secret Sauce droplets on his lips. "I'm working on myself."

She kissed him. Things here were changing, too. He loved her. Love? Had he even given that a thought lately?

The small bottle of Secret Sauce was quickly finished as he used it on everything he ate, including morning toast. He needed more sauce. After work, Richard rushed to the pop-up location.

"I need to buy more sauce." His mouth was dry, and he felt fear tightening his jaw. What if the vendor was sold out, and he had no more?

The man handed Richard another bottle after he pointed to his selection. "That'll be $100."

The price of a hundred dollars shocked Richard to the point where he almost lost his breath. "A hundred? The last time I bought it from you, it only cost one dollar."

"True. But the sauce has transformed your entire existence. Right? You aren't the same with it?"

Richard stuttered before speaking. "Yes, but why the markup?"

The vendor shrugged. "You were desperate. A person who's drowning never disputes the price with the guy who saves him."

Richard wanted to argue about the price, but he also wanted to maintain his happy demeanor with his neighbors and keep Simone in love and enjoy the incredible taste of his food instead of eating reheated cardboard. He used his credit card despite all logical financial reasons against it. Looking at the receipt, he noticed he had bought "medical supplies" from a home-delivery service.

The bottle sat on his kitchen counter as he gazed at it with a mixture of confusion. He couldn't bring himself to use the product. The cost of $100 for a condiment seemed outrageous to him. He brooded. Was he better? Or just sauced?

Two days passed before he noticed the vendor using a dolly to bring crates from the back entrance of Crescent Foods, which operated as an industrial sauce plant nearby.

Richard walked up to a supervisor at the facility because he was both curious and resentful.

Why was his Secret Sauce vendor there now?

The supervisor pointed to the man and said, "Oh, him? He buys our house-brand sauce. We put a special herb in it. Some people think it has special powers. Who knows? He buys it by the gallon, then puts a different label on it before selling it. You can get the same thing at any supermarket for two dollars a jar. He sells his in squeeze bottles to be different."

Richard stood there expecting either a revelation or a fatal heart attack to occur. The supervisor smirked. Yeah, he knew what the guy was doing. The power of the sauce was in how you believed in its effects, and this guy knew how to sell it.

Walking home with a heavy heart, Richard looked at the expensive bottle that sat on his kitchen counter. He stared at the store brand in the fridge, which he had neglected for months, as if it were taunting him. If condiments could talk, he knew this one would really give him a scolding.

What to do? He let out a deep breath before opening the inexpensive jar to taste its contents with a spoon. The flavor was uninteresting and sour, with a faint taste he couldn't identify.

At that moment, he realized something about the consequences of his actions and smiled despite everything. Mrs. Kravitz would spend her time outside tending to her geraniums as she usually did. Simone would probably contact him during the evening hours. The skateboard kid continued his daily routine of passing by the house. The sauce didn't create any of these experiences because he had changed, not them.

There was a mix of sadness and happiness. The still-swirling contents of the $100 bottle were dumped down the drain.

The cardboard taste of his dinner didn't stop him from eating it while smiling.

Fritzy

From the beginning, Fritzy carried the word failure as a persistent burr that stuck to his fur. The training facility recorded his evaluation as "Not suitable for guide work" because he displayed excessive distraction and he would puff out his chest when another dog stared at him too long. He wasn't going to finish his training after only a few weeks of testing in the field, and was deemed unsuitable by the training center to be a guide dog. But the Johnsons saw past his uncoordinated body, his pleading eyes, and his enthusiastic tail wagging when they welcomed him into their home. He may have been a failure at the center, but here he was the main attraction.

The first day of his new life ended with Fritzy almost knocking down Ellie as he ran wildly through the yard. She embraced his muscular neck while laughing. The toddler Sam sat on the porch while he shouted "doggy!" as he watched Fritzy. Rachel rested against the railing. In her third pregnancy she was tired and feeling a bit worn out. Mark scratched Fritzy's ears while the dog's warm breath touched his hand as the dog sniffed him.

Fritzy adapted to his new existence with rapid speed. He allowed Sam to pull his tail without resistance while he lay under Ellie's desk during her coloring time and followed Rachel when she carried laundry across the lawn. The dog spent his evenings lying across the hall-way with his paws resting on his chin while he watched over the children's bedrooms.

The Johnsons resided on a large property that extended past the town limits, while their white boundary fence extended into the forest. The woods beyond their property line became home to coyotes. When their distant howls reached closer to their home, Mark only shrugged. "The fence will hold," Rachel spoke softly about the coyotes' increasing boldness. Fritzy's constant back-and-forth movements across the floor indicated a different reality.

Several people in the neighborhood did not appreciate the presence of this dog. The neighbor observed Fritzy protecting Ellie from the road by placing his body between her and the asphalt while commenting about his large size. Rachel smiled at the comment while thinking to herself that "Big is exactly what I want."

Fritzy became more alert whenever he detected the presence of unfamiliar people. A deep growling sound emerged from his chest when a clipboard-carrying man approached their porch. The man stopped in his tracks while his half-smile dropped from his face. The man quickly turned around and left the property after saying, "Wrong house." Rachel reached out to touch Fritzy's head. "Good boy."

The summer season brought an atmosphere of worry, which built up like storm clouds in the air. The coyotes spent longer periods near the property boundaries while their eyes sparkled in the evening light. While offering "odd jobs", men with slick smile on display drove a rickety truck in the neighborhood. Rachel noticed how one of the men kept staring at Ellie and Sam. Fritzy detected the same thing. His posture became rigid as he produced a low growling sound from his throat. Mark described Fritzy as overly protective. Rachel had doubts about his assessment.

The test occurred on a hot Saturday afternoon. The baby lay inside while Rachel worked on settling him down. The screen door swung open as Ellie and Sam rushed outside while Fritzy followed them.

The truck approached the area at a slow pace. Two men stood by the truck speaking in sugary tones. "Hey kids! Do you want to see puppies? We have a puppy in our truck that you can see."

Ellie froze while she gripped her brother's hand tightly. Sam looked at the situation with confusion. Fritzy stepped forward to block their path toward the fence while his fur stood on end.

And then—the other threat. Movement along the treeline. The coyotes approached the area moving closer because they sensed food scraps. The coyotes displayed their yellow eyes while their bodies remained low to the ground with hungry expressions.

A single moment of time froze as children found themselves trapped between the approaching human threat at the fence and the approaching wild predators from the woods. Then Fritzy erupted.

His loud bark split through the air with the force of a rifle blast. Fritzy attacked the fence with his chest while his teeth showed in a fierce display that made Ellie jump in surprise. The men quickly retreated into their truck while using profanity as they sped away. The engine made a rough sound while the tires kicked up pieces of gravel. Gone. Fritzy continued his attack by turning toward the coyotes as he became a powerful ball of fury. His loud growls echoed throughout the grassy terrain. A close snap of his jaws forced one of the coyotes to flee into the woods. The pack stopped for a moment before they ran away, disappearing into the forest.

The area became completely quiet. Ellie collapsed in fear, and she fell onto Fritzy while her tears streamed down his fur. She wept while telling him, "You protected us from them." Sam joined in with his high-pitched voice to repeat, "Fritzy saved us!" His voice broke yet he spoke with proud determination.

Rachel rushed out of the house while holding her baby in her arms. She took a deep breath when she saw the deserted road and the fading dust and the frightened children hugging the dog. She fell to the ground to embrace all of them tightly. Her gaze met Fritzy's eyes. His eyes displayed absolute dedication without any hint of failure.

Mark listened to the story while keeping his jaw clenched. He placed his hands on Fritzy's wide shoulders as he knelt in front of the dog. "The test that really matters, you have successfully completed, buddy." Fritzy positioned his body against Mark while his tail moved back and forth across the floor.

Ellie made a crown from construction paper, which she colored gold with an uneven jewel. Then, she performed a formal ceremony to place the crown on Fritzy's head. The children said he was their hero king. The paper crown on his head seemed like solid iron to him as he displayed his proud posture with his chest forward.

Word spread. The men never returned, the coyotes stayed in the forest, and the neighbors who used to call him "big dog" now showed him respect. The neighbor approached Rachel with a simple "Good dog" statement, which made her smile.

The children, Ellie and Sam, went to sleep with Fritzy on the porch while the stars shone in the night sky. The crown slipped off his head while he slept. A firefly settled onto the crown, producing a weak light. Rachel sat on the swing with Mark while thinking about the failure label that used to be on Fritzy's identification documents.

Fritzy proved to be flawless at this moment because his family members slept peacefully under his watch.

Coffeepot Countdown

T he office coffeepot had always been a silent ally in Maggie's daily battle against spreadsheets, meetings, and her boss's endless monologues about "synergy." But today, the pot was more than a caffeine dispenser. Today, it was a countdown clock.

It started at 9:02 a.m., when the intern, Kyle, made coffee and whispered to Maggie, "Don't drink it. Someone spiked it." His wide eyes darted left and right before he scurried off toward the copier.

Maggie blinked at the glass carafe, where dark liquid sat innocently. "Spiked?" she mouthed to herself. With what? Vodka? Laxatives? Truth serum? Her imagination galloped.

She stared at the pot as if it were a live grenade. And then the line formed.

Carol from accounting waddled up first, mug in hand. "Don't you dare," Maggie hissed.

Carol arched a brow. "What's your problem?"

Maggie improvised. "New... cleaning cycle. Descaler. Toxic fumes. Probably lethal."

Carol recoiled, muttering, "Figures. Mondays," and shuffled away.

At 9:17 a.m., Frank from HR strode up, phone glued to his ear, ready to pour. Maggie blocked him with her body.

"Out of order," she barked.

Frank frowned. "It's coffee, not a printer."

"Company policy. Section... uh... seven."

Frank squinted suspiciously, then shrugged and wandered off.

By 9:32 a.m., Maggie realized she was now the sole guardian of the poisoned pot. And like every thriller protagonist ever, she had no idea what she was up against.

Kyle reappeared, clutching a folder like it contained nuclear launch codes. "It's not what you think," he whispered.

"Then what is it?" Maggie demanded.

He shook his head. "Not here. Too many ears." And he vanished again.

Her paranoia skyrocketed. Was this corporate sabotage? Industrial espionage? She thought of the rival company across town—ExcelTek, notorious for stealing clients and once, allegedly, an entire copier machine.

At 10:05 a.m., her boss, Mr. Lawrence, marched toward the pot. "Move aside, Maggie. Need my rocket fuel."

Panic surged. "Sir, you can't."

His eyes narrowed. "Why not?"

Her mind blanked. Then inspiration struck. "Because the coffee is... decaf."

A hush fell over the office. Decaf was blasphemy. Mr. Lawrence recoiled as if she'd slapped him. "Decaf?" He glared at the pot. "Unthinkable. Get rid of it."

Maggie sighed in relief as he stormed off.

By 11:00 a.m., whispers spread. "Something's wrong with the coffee," coworkers murmured. Rumors mutated: poisoned beans, mold, conspiracy. Maggie's legend grew. She was the Coffee Sentinel.

Finally, Kyle slipped her a note: "Meet in the stairwell at noon."

Maggie spent the next hour imagining every worst-case scenario. At 11:59, she left the pot unguarded for the first time all morning and crept into the stairwell.

Kyle stood two flights down, pale and jittery. "It's not poison," he confessed. "It's... experimental."

"Experimental what?"

"Product test. My uncle works at a biotech startup. They've developed a compound that makes people incapable of lying for three hours. I thought it would be funny to put it in the office coffee."

Maggie gasped. "Funny? Half this office lies for a living!"

They both froze as a scream echoed from the break room.

They rushed back to find chaos. Carol was shouting, "I fudge expense reports!" Frank wailed, "I don't recycle!" Someone else sobbed, "I've been stealing pens since 2009!"

Mr. Lawrence clutched his chest. "I don't even know what synergy means!"

The room dissolved into confessions, loud and uncontrollable. The "poisoned" coffee had done its work.

Maggie grabbed Kyle by the collar. "How much did you put in?"

"Uh... all of it?"

She buried her face in her hands. The office was now a confessional booth on steroids.

By 3:00 p.m., the truth serum wore off. Silence blanketed the office. No one made eye contact. The coffeepot sat empty, a glassy monument to chaos.

Mr. Lawrence emerged from his office, eyes bloodshot. He cleared his throat. "Staff meeting. Tomorrow. Early. Bring coffee. From Starbucks."

No one objected.

Maggie slumped at her desk, exhausted. Kyle whispered, "See? It wasn't so bad."

She glared at him. "Kyle, you turned this place into a reality show without cameras."

And yet, she smiled faintly. Under the embarrassment, something lingered: relief. Secrets had spilled, lies had cracked, and oddly, people looked a little freer.

As the office lights dimmed, Maggie poured the last drop of cold, cursed coffee into her mug. She raised it in a toast to survival.

"To the coffeepot countdown," she murmured. "May it never return."

Appendix A —The Official HR Memo

To: All Staff

From: Human Resources

Subject: Prohibition of Experimental Beverages in the Workplace

It has come to management's attention that unauthorized substances were introduced into the communal coffeepot on Monday morning. While the resulting confessions did provide unusual insight into employee behavior, it is the official stance of HR that truth serums, laxatives, or other "experimental enhancements" are not appropriate office additives.

Effective immediately:

1. Only approved coffee, tea, or water may be placed in shared appliances.

2. Any employee found tampering with the coffee supply will be required to attend a seminar titled "Ethics in the Break Room."

3. Starbucks gift cards will be distributed on Fridays to prevent future sabotage.

We thank you for your cooperation in keeping our workplace both caffeinated and sane.

Appendix B – Anonymous Employee Comments

"Honestly, it was the best staff meeting we've ever had."

"I can't believe Frank admitted he doesn't recycle. I'll never look at him the same way."

"Confessing about stealing pens was liberating. I may go to Staples now, guilt-free."

"I hope Kyle never makes coffee again."

Sole Stories

U nder the moonlit sky with drifting clouds the world remained silent except for the silent whispers that only invisible listeners heard through frayed and dirty laces. The pink satin ballet slipper had lost its pristine hue. A worn-out red shoe rests against its partner while it releases hushed words into the damp air showing of past dancing movements that will never happen again.

The worn leather boot that had a cloak of mud on its surface shared its story about how her little girl named all the stars that appeared in the sky. She spent each evening in the yard warming her feet while teaching her younger sister about the stars' names by pointing them out in the sky.

The small brown sandal, which lost its buckle, pushed against the boot forced closer by the pile's weight while it yearned to share its summer memories of skipping stones across the pond. A joyful clap and jump came from the wearer after seven bounces, a stone skipping record. The buckle of the shoe came loose during that time spent in the garden with her mother while singing to make vegetables grow.

The wooden clog with faded painted tulips remains silent about its owner who wore silver embroidery on his slippers, memories of play-ing chess with a grandfather through its unfinished Queen's Gambit game on a solitary board. The house stands vacant because its windows are shattered and its front door hangs from a broken hinge.

The pile of shoes contained many voices which blended together to share their memories of playing soccer in town and performing double Dutch jump rope while their braids moved to counting songs.

When thunder started rumbling above, the thousands of shoes didn't react. The pair of winter boots located high in the pile showed their deep snow memories through their fur lining which had become matted and torn while they whispered motivation during each step. The raindrops hit the shoes but the stories kept flowing as precious secrets in the darkness.

The cloth sneaker with a hole in its toe shared stories about spending time in meadows drawing wildflowers while dreaming about becoming a well-known artist. A patent leather shoe with cracks and a lost shine kept the memory of a six-candle birthday cake and an unspoken wish. The conversations during the night revealed interrupted lives and frozen childhood moments which remained as permanent as album pictures.

The leather Oxford shoe now shows scuffs on its surface while its metal buckle continues to reflect light as it moves through the pile. It knew the chambermaid received complaints from him about her inadequate polishing work for his piano performances.

A work boot with a separated sole and a tired appearance emerged from the pile to respond with a soft voice. "The boy didn't complain about his cold toes during winter because he had given his socks to his sister."

The Oxford remains quiet for a brief instant. "We share the exact same dimensions as each other."

The work boot responds with a statement about following different life paths. "Until now."

The Oxford reveals something about his boy, "He wept the first time when he damaged me."

The work boot subtly indicated its owner's feelings, only shedding a tear once when the authorities confiscated his father's boots.

A brisk wind swept across the top of the pile sending two shoes falling while rearranging several others. The Oxford shifted its position while its leather made a creaking sound as it remembered walking across the marble floors of the villa during drawing room events. The work boot displayed cobblestone street marks and market day scars on its cracked leather while its patches told the story of candlelit repairs.

The work boot's loose sole moved again as another gust of wind brushed the pile and it signaled rain was approaching. "Mine helped, too. The boy spent his early mornings at dawn assisting his father during potato cart loading duties. The boy walked fourteen steps from the cart to the cellar while working six hours daily."

"Different music," the Oxford noted.

The work boot agreed that their musical experiences were distinct from each other. A Mozart melody came from the violin while he worked with his humming. The song existed in both places but the musicians performed it in separate locations.

The Oxford's commanding voice became more rigid during that moment. "The street children outside our window used to fascinate his son."

The work boot had observed the son watching through his window. "I felt the violin produced heavenly sounds." The two remained silent after that moment when they found themselves side by side on the same ground. The Oxford and the work boots experience a shared moment of unity as they pressed against each other in the dark while the yard's mud created their common ground.

A loud truck engine with a harsh coughing sound interrupted their memories as headlights illuminated the enormous pile of shoes. The workers started placing shoes and boots into the worn wheelbarrow and the flatbed truck. Brief views of their buildings were seen before the dawn rose. The voice from inside the pile spoke its final words before the truck disappeared into the distance: "We carried them as far as we could."

The truck wheels created waves in the puddles while navigating through the muddy turn on its path toward the city. To the rising sun, the pair of tiny red boots with metal fasteners whispered, "We remember. The memories and stories we carry will stay with us forever." Everything was quiet. Even the rain had stopped.

The dark gray wooden buildings created a shadowed area that the morning sun gradually cleared by dissolving the remaining clouds from the yard. Briefly, it illuminated the sign that hung between barbed wire fencing at the entrance of the yard. Serving a dual purpose, the sign promised and memorialized with the words "Arbeitmacht frei," meaning "Work sets you free."

Water on the Side

S altines with a plain glass of water and a slice of lemon on the side were all that faced Sarah. Her fingers tapped an unconscious rhythm against the coffee shop table—a Morse code of hunger matched by her hollow stomach. The Saltines before her had the appeal of cardboard, but she forced one between her lips, letting it dissolve. Her throat constricted between each dry swallow.

Her old laptop with sheet music poking out of a side pocket was propped against the table leg. Sitting there, she might have been a minor painting in someone's collection, but today, she sat and waited in this small coffee shop on the city's west side. For what reason or who was she waiting for? Could anybody guess, or would they have the temerity to ask? No one would interfere with her reverie, and she would be left to muse alone. Waiting alone was something she'd become accustomed to.

Sarah hunched over the free water and packet of Saltines—her last food until tomorrow's advance from her sister, a successful computer engineer, arrived. Her mother's voice reverberated in her head. "You've got to go to college and major in computers like your sister," she kept repeating. But Sarah wanted to write music, and no one in the family understood.

Untouched, the lemon slice snuck from the condiment station lay next to the glass. Lemons and water were one way to keep your weight down, as she had learned from her tumultuous youth. Her mother had screamed, too, about weight, yet she always stressed that everyone clean their dinner plates. The contradiction never seemed to bother h er.

As Sarah sat alone and silent, her apartment key dug into her hip through her thin jeans. It was a constant reminder of the rent-controlled fifth-floor walkup she might lose if something didn't change soon.

Earlier, three rejection emails had glowed on her laptop screen, their corporate syrupy pleasantries echoing in her mind: "Not quite what we're looking for," "Doesn't fit our current roster," and "Keep developing your craft."

Almost unnoticed, standing off to the side near the front door, was a guy in a corduroy jacket who appeared during this mid-afternoon lull. Without speaking, he approached her and slipped a cream-colored business card next to her water glass. The distinctive font read: "Robert Rowdy, Melody Finder (When you're ready to listen)." On the reverse side, precise handwriting read: "Corner of 12th and Pine. Tomorrow. 3 PM." No words were spoken, and he slipped out the front door.

The following day, she threw caution to the wind and walked toward the shop as though through driven snow. The record store's darkness somehow enveloped her in a comforting sense of stability. Dust specks pirouetted in narrow sunbeams that sliced through weathered blinds, dancing to their silent symphony. Album covers lined the walls in faded glory, their musty-sweet scent mixing with the oiled-wood smell of old shelving.

Working at the front desk, each time Robert lifted a needle on a record, the speaker's static crackled like distant thunder before the music began. Her nostrils flared at the familiar scent of vinyl—fresh yet old mingling together.

For two hours, he played snippets, never explaining, just watching her reactions and taking notes. Then came the catch. The homework he assigned was in clipped phrases with a mandate to study ten songs—required equipment she didn't have. When she mentioned her broken equipment, her voice cracked like a warped record. Marcus's shoulders stiffened, his hand freezing mid-reach for another album. The silence stretched between them like an out-of-tune string until he turned to the counter.

But then he paused, seemed to think a minute, and pulled out a battered Walkman-type unit and headphones from beneath the counter. "Return these when you've made something true," he said. "Not something you think will sell. Something that's yours." He hesitated, then added, "The studio upstairs records demos on Sundays. Be here at five p.m. next week. One song, one take."

The fire escape became her urban orchestra pit. Five stories below, taxi horns punctuated the bass line of idling engines. Rain tapped steel in syncopated rhythms while distant sirens wailed their lonely soprano. Through Robert's headphones, global rhythms merged with her city's symphony, birthing something new. The music was there, but it was so beautifully hidden by her inability to hear it.

That Sunday, she climbed the narrow stairs above the record shop to find a small but professional studio. Robert sat at the board while a sound engineer she'd never seen before set up a microphone. "One take," Robert reminded her. Make it count."

After its completion, without her knowledge, the sound engineer gave the demo to the indie label where he also worked. It caught the right ear. The advance wasn't much, but it covered rent and a decent microphone for her computer. More importantly, it stopped her from chasing what others wanted to hear.

Her fingers found their way to her laptop keys and music notation program, typing in time with the squeaking stairs below, footsteps echoing up all five flights, and the pigeons cooing on her windowsill. Each sound wove into her city's endless song. The same coffee shop where Robert had found her now played her latest track—she'd heard it yesterday while ordering an actual meal, her royalty check still safe in her pocket.

A new workbench beckoned to her, and Sarah moved to her fire escape. She returned Robert's Walkman months ago, along with the sheet music for the demo, which became her breakthrough song.

The sunset painted the city in amber and rose, and somewhere in the maze of buildings, another artist sat alone with only water and crackers, waiting for their moment. She pulled out her phone and sent a quick text to Robert: "Find someone who needs to listen differently. It's your turn to work your magic again."

The city's symphony swelled around her—the rhythmic thump of someone dragging a heavy box upstairs, children's laughter floating up from the street, a saxophone wailing from an open window three buildings over—no longer noise but possibility. She smiled, knowing that creativity, like sound itself, was just a matter of learning to tune in to what was always there.

Forever Silk Flowers

"Miriam, you have to eat something." Her mother gave her a thick slice of bread and pushed it onto her plate. Miriam felt uncomfortable with the comment and hid the bread in her jacket. She was already late for her shift.

The factory smelled terrible when she walked in; glue and chemicals were strongly scented. Miriam was twelve, and like many poor children, she was dressed in hand-me-down clothes and worked on the production floor of the factory. People had no issue with Miriam's situation after her father's death.

"Hurry, girl," Mrs. Peterson told her from the next station. "The hat flowers need to be completed and delivered to the millinery by five o'clock."

When sitting down at her bench, Miriam's fingers moved quickly across the cotton and silk to create the roses, the tiny forget-me-nots, and other flowers used to adorn the hats of ladies. Her sisters, Elena and Marie, worked three floors up making the leaves, while Ana, who was just seven, stayed home with Mama, who took in washing when her cough permitted.

The assembly line was quiet, and the only sounds were a few words in different languages spoken by immigrant girls who had come to America to achieve their dreams.

"Did you hear?" Maria asked her and her friends during their water break. "They're bringing in something new. Special orders from the department stores."

Miriam paid little attention to the conversation. Her hands were sore from the rough dyes, and she couldn't increase her pace. Winter was coming, and they needed coal for the stove.

"Attention!" the floor manager, Mr. Barnes, barked. "We have a new product line, ladies. High-end stuff."

Boxes appeared at each station, filled with delicate silk and velvet that Miriam had never seen before. The weak sunlight from the overhead windows illuminated the deep colors and cast shadows like paintings across her workspace.

Barnes smiled in a curious way, his lips curled. "These need to be perfect. They're for a spring window display. Mess them up; it comes out of your pay."

The workers grumbled as a group, but Miriam's heart beat fast. The rich fabrics took her back to the shop window curtains Papa used to point out on their Sunday walks.

"What's the matter, kid?" Barnes noticed her hesitation. "The stuff is too fancy for you?"

Miriam shook her head, and what Papa said came back to her: 'Beauty is all around, even in the simplest of things. She looked at the sample flower and saw that the petals had to catch the light in a certain way.

By lunch, Miriam had 20 perfect specimens, while the rest struggled with the delicate material. Each one looked almost real, and it glittered like garden flowers in the early morning dew.

"How did you do that?" asked Barnes, looking at her work.

"It's in how you fold them," Miriam explained quietly. "It's like how real flowers face the sun."

That evening, when she was climbing the five flights up to their tenement apartment, Miriam's feet ached from the walking. Her mother's cough and the smell of boiled cabbage and potatoes greeted her.

"Barnes offered me a new position," Miriam told her family over dinner as she watched her sisters divide the meager portions. "I am teaching others how to make fancy flowers. A dollar more a week, Mama."

Her mother's eyes became teary. "Your papa would be so proud. But your hands..."

That Sunday, at Papa's grave, Miriam placed one of her silk flowers by the stone. "Look, Papa," she said, pulling something from her pocket, his old journal where he used to sketch designs for the furniture he dreamed of making. "I'm using it like you showed me."

She had been filling the blank pages with flower designs, with each petal drawn separately, and notes on how to shape them and which materials to use for each. The work supervisor saw her sketches and told her to come up with new patterns for the spring line.

That night, by candlelight, Miriam drew her last design as her sisters slept. The next day, she stood before a group of workers, mostly young girls like herself, and taught them how to force beauty from simple materials.

Barnes gave her a small desk near the window where she could sketch and plan during teaching sessions. Every design she made, every girl she trained, seemed like a step away from the grinding poverty that filled their tenement halls. Now, they could buy a bit more coal and a little meat this week.

When night came early in winter, Miriam gathered her precious journal and pulled her thin shawl closer. She would go back tomorrow and shape more flowers, but now each one was more than just a way to earn bread. In her father's journal, her flower designs came to life, alongside his furniture sketches, and they became a growing portfolio that could one day lead to better things.

Standing at the door as the darkness gathered, she stopped to look at the bright department store windows. Her flowers and designs would be a part of these displays soon. Maybe one day, she thought, it would be her name up there, not just as a factory girl but as an artist.

The Lighthouse Keeper's Watch

The lighthouse had stood for more than a century on the edge of the headland, its white tower battered by salt and wind. Tourists came in summer, snapping photos and climbing the spiral steps, but in winter it was left to Arthur, the keeper, and the long hours of waiting between storms.

Arthur had been the keeper for thirty years, though "keeper" now was more a title of nostalgia. Automated bulbs flashed on a schedule, the foghorn bellowed when sensors told it to. His job was maintenance, reporting, and most of all, presence. Someone had to live here, to keep watch. Or so the agency said.

He rose before dawn, made coffee strong enough to chip enamel, and logged the weather. Then he walked the gallery, his boots echoing against the iron stairs. He checked the beam, though it needed no checking, wiped dust from brass that tarnished anyway, and stood at the window looking at an empty horizon.

Waiting, always waiting. For storms, for ships, for the unexpected knock of fate. He'd be there doing his job just as he always had.

Once, ships had needed him. He remembered the night a freighter listed dangerously, and he had guided rescue boats through a channel of jagged teeth. Another time, a fishing trawler had sent its last may-day, and the crew was saved because his lamp had burned steady. He remembered the faces of those he'd pulled half-drowned from the sea, coughing, crying, clinging to him. Back then, waiting had purpose.

Now, most days passed without a vessel in sight. Technology had outpaced him. Yet he stayed.

At night he wrote letters he never sent—to his late wife, to the daughter who had grown and gone to the city, to the ocean itself. The papers stacked on his desk like shells washed ashore, silent, unfinished. He wondered if words cast into silence ever reached anyone.

One December evening, a storm rose quickly. Clouds swallowed the horizon, and the sea hurled itself against the rocks. Arthur stood at the window, his heart thudding with the old alertness. He climbed to the beacon room, checked the rotation, listened to the foghorn's mournful cry. Hours passed. No ships appeared.

At midnight, a faint light flickered in the distance. Arthur pressed binoculars to his eyes. A small boat, too small for the open sea, tossed violently in the waves. His pulse surged. He radioed the coast guard, but interference made the line static. He cursed, grabbed his raincoat, and hurried down the cliff path.

The wind shoved against him, tearing at his hood. Spray blinded him, but he kept moving, lantern held high. On the rocks below, the boat slammed and splintered. A figure clung to the wreckage—a boy, barely more than sixteen, his face pale in the lightning's flash.

Arthur waded in, the surf crashing to his waist. He seized the boy's arm, pulling him free as the sea tried to swallow them both. With a final heave, he dragged him onto the rocks. The boy coughed seawater, shivering violently.

"Easy, lad. You're safe."

The boy blinked up at him, dazed. "The light... I followed the light."

Arthur felt his throat tighten. "That's what it's there for."

They climbed back to the tower. Arthur wrapped him in blankets, brewed tea, and listened as the boy explained. He'd stolen the boat on a dare, wanting to prove himself. When the storm hit, he thought he was finished. "Then I saw your beam," he said. "It was like it was waiting just for me."

Arthur sat across from him, the words sinking in. Waiting just for me. All those empty nights, all the hours spent alone, suddenly condensed into this single moment. He realized the waiting had never been wasted. It had been an offering, a vigil for whoever needed it.

The boy slept in the cot, breathing steadily. Arthur returned to the gallery, the storm easing at last. He leaned on the railing, gazing at the horizon where faint stars reappeared. His watch had mattered, after a ll.

He reached for the stack of letters on his desk, took a fresh sheet, and began to write—not to the sea, not to silence, but to his daughter. He wrote of storms, of rescues, of waiting that was never empty. He wrote so she would know that light endures, even when no one seems to see it.

When the dawn came, gold spilling across the water, Arthur was still writing. The boy stirred, alive because the light had waited. And Arthur, keeper of the watch, no longer doubted the worth of his vigil.

Shifting Sands

S arah's hands shook while she completed the last mortgage document. The wedding ring on her hand reflected the sunlight that entered the realtor's office through the window. Mark placed his hand on her shoulder to calm her racing heartbeat.

The realtor handed them the deed with a cheerful welcome to Sandpiper Isle after they signed the document. "Welcome to Sandpiper Isle."

The house stood elevated on stilts as the November sky merged with its weathered gray shingles while the dunes formed frozen waves beneath it. The sea breeze made the sea oats bend as waves continuously whispered against the shore.

Mark spoke his words with a shaking voice when he said, "We did it." The entire sum of their savings and 401ks and his mother's inheritance went toward their dream of owning a beachfront property.

The couple spent their inaugural evening in their new house on the deck to watch the moon create silver lines across the Atlantic Ocean. The house made its presence known through creaks and settling movements as the constant ocean waves created the soothing sounds Sarah had always wanted to experience during her Outer Banks childhood vacations.

Three weeks later, the letter arrived.

Sarah read the letter from the property owner to herself as her coffee grew cold on the kitchen counter. "The State Geological Survey has discovered major coastal erosion patterns on Sandpiper Isle which might impact your property ownership."

Mark took the letter from her hand while his expression turned dark as he studied the official State Geological Survey letterhead.

As planned even before knowing about this turn of events, the couple wanted an expert to look over their property—just to be sure. Dr. Eleanor Adams entered their living room to present colorful topographical maps on her tablet. Her rimmed glasses failed to conceal the compassionate expression she showed them.

The western section of the barrier island maintains stability according to her explanation as she zoomed in on their location. "But this section?" She pointed to their street with her finger. "The area shows the highest rates of erosion that have never been observed before. The sand foundation beneath the surface shows warning signs of structural weakness."

Sarah tightened her grip on the chair back until her knuckles turned white while asking about the implications for their residence.

The best possible outcome would result in five years before major structural problems emerge. Dr. Adams shifted her glasses before delivering the most severe prediction. A major storm could destroy the foundation of the house completely.

Mark walked back and forth in the room while his footsteps echoed across the hardwood floors, which they had already decided to refinish. The inspection results must contain an error because this couldn't be true. "There must be some mistake. The inspection-"

"Standard home inspections fail to include deep geological surveys," according to Dr. Adams, who delivered the information with care. "I'm sorry."

The waves that brought Sarah peace earlier now sounded like predators to her during her sleepless night. The sound of them transformed into a menacing growl that made her picture the sand disappearing beneath their home while they slept.

The following months passed quickly while they sought professional advice. The engineers proposed several reinforcement solutions which exceeded the price they originally paid for their house. The insurance adjusters denied their claims because they found "pre-existing conditions" in the property. The real estate lawyers discussed disclosure regulations and previous survey results in controlled language which failed to bring them any comfort.

Their dream house evolved into an anxious trap that made them lie awake during every storm. Sarah marked the distance between their house steps and the dune line using driftwood pieces to measure the space between their present and potential disaster.

Mark dedicated his free time to studying coastal erosion reports and geological data about the area. The experts they consulted through their dwindling savings confirmed Dr. Adams' first assessment while their financial resources continued to decrease.

Then came the nor'easter.

The storm brought three days of intense wind that pounded against the dunes with the force of heavy clubs. They left their home to stay in a motel while they spent restless nights thinking about their house sinking into the ocean.

But despite their fears, the house maintained its original condition after their departure. It was upright on its stilts without any damage to its shingles.

Mark looked at their dwindling savings account before suggesting they should sell their house during that evening. "We should sell the property now because we can still realize some value from it," Sarah mumbled as the sunset transformed the ocean waves into golden and coral hues. "But the knowledge we have makes it impossible to understand who would purchase this property."

The second correspondence reached their mailbox during the seventh month following the initial letter.

The letter started with "Mr. and Mrs. Davidson," before Dr. Adams signed it with her signature at the end. The letter became difficult to read because Sarah's hands were shaking uncontrollably.

Mark approached her from behind to embrace her waist while they read the letter together.

The letter explained that geological surveys after the first letter showed an uncharted granite sill which runs beneath the western part of Sandpiper Isle. "The formation exists at a depth of forty feet beneath the surface which provides strong structural support to the area. The previous erosion predictions were incorrect because they relied on insufficient data."

Sarah faced Mark while her face streamed with tears as she asked if they were safe.

The granite structure had been present since the beginning to protect them from danger, according to his tearful confirmation.

The couple drank champagne on their deck that night. They'd bought it for the closing but chose not to open it because of their anxiety. Now the ocean waves continued to whisper, but Sarah heard their melody as a joyful celebration instead of a warning.

Mark held his glass to toast the rock which supports the sand as the moonlight sparkled through the champagne bubbles.

Sarah tapped her glass against his while standing on the solid foundation of their house. The existence of ancient stone formed an eternal foundation beneath their dream house. It was a miracle.

She took down the driftwood markers from the dune line the following day so the tide could sweep them away. She planted sea oats and beach roses in their garden because their roots descended toward the hidden foundation which had been present since the beginning.

Through it all, Sarah shared their entire experience of fear and doubt with new neighbors who moved into the area. The survey marker, a small metal disc, demonstrated how the earth contains secrets that can't be seen.

The house continued to produce creaking and settling noises during storms, yet Sarah found joy in the sounds. The old wood spoke to the wind through its sounds as it shared secrets with the waves. The granite foundation maintained its permanent position while the sand above it continued to shift. But it was home and they were safe.

After the Storm

M ark's coffee mug dropped to the floor when he received the development company letter. "They're planning what?"

Sarah quickly read the paper before taking it from him. The development plan included a high-rise resort complex which required all beachfront property owners to sell their land through eminent domain procedures.

Their granite foundation-based home became exposed to a new danger which emerged five years after their initial discovery. The same granite sill which protected their property from damage proved ideal for Coastal Ventures LLC to build their large-scale development project.

The next day Dr. Eleanor Adams appeared with her usual scientific composure but displayed an air of emergency. The research data about granite formation which she provided to them now served as the basis for their development plans.

Sarah asked if the developers had the power to force property owners to sell their land.

"The economic growth of the island serves as their basis for claiming ownership of the land," according to Eleanor. The granite structure of this area makes it the only feasible location for constructing large-scale developments.

The community members who lived there united as one force. Amy dedicated herself to research after completing her geology studies. The granite formation supported a distinct ecological system that protected multiple endangered bird and marine species.

Mark used their living room to host community meetings while Sarah worked with environmental organizations. The house which used to cause them stress now served as the central base for their fight against the development.

The development company made progressively more forceful real estate proposals to the owners. The representative from the development company presented them with a fivefold increase of their original purchase price while standing on the deck where they had previously celebrated their granite discovery. "You can find a different location on the coastline." And just like that, he thought they'd sell and leave.

Sarah stated that they wanted to stay in their current location.

Amy and Dr. Adams discovered vital climate change research minerals within the granite formation through their late-night core sample analysis. Here was a glimmer of hope.

"The scientific value of this site exceeds the worth of building a resort because it holds essential information about coastal adaptation to sea level rise," according to Dr. Adams during the county hearing. "The scientific community recognizes this formation as a vital discovery for studying coastal area adaptation to sea level rise. The research potential alone..."

The scientific community united to support the cause. Research universities presented their funding proposals to the authorities. The scientific community filed environmental protection orders with the authorities.

A new letter arrived three months later, which established the area as a National Scientific Reserve. The development plans received their final death sentence.

The evening brought Sarah and Mark to their deck for a celebration again but time with Dr. Adams who raised her glass. "The granite formation protected our home twice and we celebrate it with this toast," Sarah almost whispered as she raised her glass.

Amy announced she had secured funding to study the formation through a grant. She would conduct her graduate studies at this location because she had received a research grant. "I'll be doing my graduate work right here," she said grinning. "I hope you don't mind when I collect core samples every month."

Sarah held Mark's hand while they watched the sun disappear over the hills. The granite foundation which initially threatened their home and later protected it now served as their lasting heritage which safeguarded their residence and all the surrounding wildlife and scientific research opportunities.

Their home evolved into something greater than a house and a saved dream protected by ancient stone. The discovery revealed a new perspective about their environment because valuable things exist in places we cannot see.

The Universe

Mark Dalton checked his watch for the third time in as many minutes. It was 8:42 AM, and his train was still delayed by 17 minutes, according to the digital display on the platform.

"This can't be happening," he muttered, walking back and forth, the soles of his polished loafers clicking against the concrete. The quarterly presentation to the board was at 9:30 sharp, and Arthur Branston, the CEO, was notorious for his punctuality. Those who arrived late weren't invited back.

A gust of autumn wind blew through the station, making a newspaper that had been lying on the ground move across the platform in a ghost-like fashion. Mark's phone was ringing.

"Where are you?" It was Sarah from accounting.

"Still at station. Train delayed. Cover for me?"

"Can't. Branston already asking."

Mark's stomach tightened. He had put in six months of hard work and countless sleepless nights, and the prospects of a promotion were all riding on the line because of a mechanical problem on the 8:25 express.

"Attention passengers," the garbled station announcement system echoed. "We apologize for the delay. The 8:25 train to Grand Central is now delayed by 23 minutes due to a signal problem."

"Twenty-three?" Mark was screaming in his head, whether in disbelief or anger, but it wasn't all in his head. It was coming out loud enough for an older woman to look up from her book. "That's—that's impossible!"

He started using his cell to look for another way to get to the office now. The rideshare pricing was through the roof. There were no available Ubers. The next train wouldn't come until after his presentation was to start.

The older woman closed her book. "You look like you're about to have a stroke."

Mark ran a hand through his hair, which he had taken such pain to style, and it tumbled. "I have a career-defining presentation in 45 minutes, and I need to be downtown for it."

She nodded. "Sometimes the universe has other plans." Her voice had a tinge of sadness in it.

"The universe can keep its plans. I need to keep my job," Mark snapped and then regretted it. "I'm sorry. That was uncalled for."

"Quite alright. I've lived long enough to know that missed trains sometimes lead to unexpected destinations." She smiled again and reopened her book.

For Mark, it was finally over, and for the next two weeks, the company faced the death of its CEO. Memorial services were held; interim leadership was put in place. During all of this, Mark started to think about the woman and her words about missing the train and arriving at some other place.

Two weeks later, Mark was called into the manager's office.

"The board met yesterday," Jim said, pointing to a seat for Mark. "Due to recent events, there has been a major staff reshuffle."

Mark nodded seriously. He knew what was coming, and he tried to prepare for it. The end wasn't going to be pretty.

"Your quarterly projections, the ones you never got to present, have been looked at. And your work on the Asian market's expansion? Apparently, Branston had made some notes about it after his Tokyo trip."

Jim handed a folder to Mark. "The board wants you to head the new Pacific Division. It's a vice presidency, Mark."

Mark stared at the folder in disbelief. "I don't know what to say."

"Sometimes being in the right place at the right time is just... destiny." Jim smiled sadly. "Or, in your case, being in the wrong place at what turned out to be exactly the right time."

That evening, getting on the train to go home, Mark noticed a person he knew standing on the platform—an older woman with a book.

"Congratulations on your new job," she said when he came closer.

Mark blinked in surprise. "How did you...?"

"I didn't," she said with a smile. "But you have that look. The look that people get when they've seen how thin the line is between disaster and fortune."

The train screeched into the station; its doors opened with a soft hissing sound.

"After you," Mark murmured as he gestured to her with his arm outstretched.

"No," she replied, her eyes shining. "I think I'll wait for the next one."

Ambition

The afternoon sunlight brought no comfort to the publishing industry's most feared critic who wrote under the pen name "the most feared woman in publishing." The sun illuminated her pale white fish-belly complexion and her red hair which resembled Brillo pads around her round face. The red lipstick she wore created an unflattering visual effect that people called makeup. Her own eyes couldn't see her appearance's disarray.

Margaret Thorne gazed at her expanding list of upcoming books while saying, "Another mound of major miracles," to herself. She had placed herself beside Gerald Matthews during the editorial meeting because his shaking hands had caused two coffee spills. One She author's name was presented to him while she made eye contact with department heads during the meeting.

The woman knew how to manipulate and she used a worried tone to inform the publisher's assistant about Gerald's submission deadline mix-up before returning to her office. She handled the book with care before placing it on her desk, her thick fingers checking the dust cover for any damage. The book and its protective dust cover needed to remain unharmed because any damage would lower its market value.

At lunch with the publisher's assistant, she steered the discussion toward retirement benefits while expressing concern about people who fail to recognize their time for retirement. Next, a policy change proposal was something she presented as a necessary improvement to editorial operations; she knew it would reach the appropriate decision-makers.

The planned rumors started spreading at the same time she had anticipated. The forty years Gerald spent serving the company would become irrelevant when doubt began to spread. He had inherited the position through family. She would take over his office space after he left in a few weeks.

The job now was to choose which books would receive positive reviews and which would receive negative ones. Scanning the colorful books on her review list, she examined the unblemished book spines on the shelves. The authors she had promoted to fame through her book reviews and written words stood before her. Yes, she had made them famous. She was, after all, the most feared woman in all of book publishing.

Through the glass partition, Amy Morrow sorted books while her shoulders slumped and her glasses moved down her nose. The four years she spent working as Margaret's assistant taught her to recognize her boss's needs before they actually appeared.

Margaret asked Amy to show her the upcoming books on her list.

Amy entered the room with her tablet in hand. A mouse of a girl, she wore a plain business suit that made her look like a timid rodent. "The new book from the author who met with you at lunch arrived at the office this morning. You know The National Book Awards is approaching and publishers are requesting review coverage from you."

"The new book should be the first item on Tuesday's reading list." A smirk came across her lips. She remembered all the young male authors who brought her to lunch hoping to receive a positive book review. She didn't need to search for young authors because they actively sought her attention. The events that followed remained private to everyone else.

The text message from Jerome at Cornerstone Books appeared on Margaret's phone. "The shipment for Tuesday needs preparation. The same conditions apply to this transaction." She typed out a fast response before grabbing her cashmere coat, the one she enjoyed throwing into the air to let it fall near the coat rack. Amy would pick it up.

"Must leave early today," she said almost over her shoulder as she moved toward the door. It was before her scheduled time.

"I need to read some material. I want all calls to be ignored until tomorrow." The security guard watched as she jostled her rolling suitcase toward the parking garage where she frequently entered the building.

The back entrance of Cornerstone Books had its familiar scent, a combination of cardboard with cigarette smoke and coffee. Jerome handled the book transfer from her suitcase to his storage area with speed while he counted out money between transfers. It was an operation that needed to finish before anyone detected it and both parties understood the situation.

Jerome whispered to her that the current selection was premium quality and the autographed item would sell quickly. She gave a half-smile while keeping her secret about the book acquisition to herself.

Margaret wanted the book transfer to occur without any noise while she stuffed her designer purse and avoided paying taxes. But this time there was one catch and it had to do with Amy, who beneath her mousy appearance held massive ambition. She managed to cell phone video the entire transfer of the books into Margaret's suitcase and it was done so expertly that she went unnoticed.

The video would serve as Amy's protection for her future career advancement to become a book reviewer. Four years of verbal abuse was about to be repaid.

The IRS agents showed up at Margaret's office during a period of several months filled with nonstop deadlines and book deliveries. Clandestine purchases of reviewer's copies of books were now into the thousands and this had been a practice of Margaret's for years.

The lead agent delivered a direct statement to Ms. Thorne when he asked her to accompany him. Margaret's voice trembled when she asked for clarification about the situation. "Amy," she yelled, ""contact legal services right away!"

Amy reached for her phone while maintaining a fake expression of shock and worry. "Right away, Ms. Thorne."

The publisher scheduled an urgent meeting with all staff members for the next morning after the arrest. He had received a warning about the upcoming event from someone who had asked him to remain anonymous.

The office space where Margaret used to work remained vacant and her meeting chair sat empty. The conference room became a space where people exchanged hushed conversations.

"It's a somber day for publishing," the publisher said. And we're going to immediately begin staffing changes to our organization. Amy felt a twinge of expectation that her plan had worked and she would be moving up in the company.

"James Parker will take over Margaret's column for the following month and, Amy will be responsible for children's book review."

Amy expressed gratitude for the opportunity through her composed voice although her dreams were shattering at that moment. The promotion to children's books didn't offer any significant career advancement. The books she reviewed lacked Maurice Sendak illustrations, so they failed to reach bestseller status, which left her in reviewer limbo.

Amy spent the evening in her apartment while reading the email that confirmed her new position. Sarah came over and knocked on Amy's door with wine and congratulations in hand.

But to Sarah's surprise, there was none of the expected happiness and relief.

"I made the correct decision" Amy asked. "Didn't I?"

"The answer depends on what you truly wanted," her friend and neighbor said.

Social media ate the story up as Margaret's duplicity became the fodder for a publishing world eager to see her brought down from her lofty perch. Two colleagues in the elevator spoke in hushed tones about Amy's decision to report Margaret to the authorities.

The news about her betrayal of his employer spread like wildfire through the office. Wasn't it supposed to be kept secret and anonymous? No, the gossip mill always finds a way.

Amy began her first children's book review at her new cubicle which lacked windows and corner office views. The display screen displayed her reflection which briefly showed Margaret's face with its intense desire for recognition and her willingness to make deals. The wallpaper on the laptop had been altered at Margaret's request and they hadn't gotten around to changing it yet.

In her apartment, Amy spent the evening at her small desk, surrounded by children's books. The HR department sent her an email through her cell phone about the following day to inform her about the magazine's restructuring plan again, which would merge her department into another editor's section within weeks. The humiliation was continuing. Instead of ascending, she was being pushed into someone else's domain and there she would linger, not thrive.

She laughed alone in the room while saying "Perfect. Just perfect."

Her resignation letter was the first thing she began inputting after she saw the HR email. She wrote with complete sincerity for the first time since becoming an adult, but was a bitterness her, too. The taste made her want a glass of water.

The desire to become Margaret had consumed her for years until she understood that the position brought no satisfaction. Corporate restructuring process now relocated her to work under another department leader as an entry-level employee. Entry level? The thought was almost too much for her to bear.

They failed to promote her into the position that Margaret held. The prize remained out of her reach and she understood that it had not been worth the sacrifices she made. The weight of guilt started to occupy her mind as it developed into a distressing mental burden.

She read the email she was sending to the publisher. In it she stated that integrity loses its value when people sell it because it can't be recovered through any purchase.

The new copy of Edgar Allan Poe's "The Tell-Tale Heart" on her bookshelf drew her attention. She purchased this book during her visit to Cornerstone Books. The book felt light in her hands but she understood its deep meaning.

The first page of the book brought back Margaret's first-day statement to her: "In this business, Amy everyone has a price to pay. The key to success lies in understanding your personal worth." Sliding the book back onto the shelf, she decided she could start her own literary legacy through review writing which would transform her reputation. There were contacts she'd made over these years and promises that she could now collect. Her entire professional life working as an assistant for others was over. The evening brought endless choices while keeping all potential remorse out of the way.

Pushing the review books aside, she started writing on her laptop while the darkness surrounded her as she typed, "The most dangerous stories are always here," with a smile because they exist within our own minds.

Waiting for Perfect

E lizabeth's fingertips left streaks on the spotless windows as she pressed against the glass. Twenty stories below, yellow cabs crawled like beetles. "The morning light here is incredible. Tom, imagine waking up to this view."

Tom wrapped his arms around her waist, his reflection ghosting against the cityscape. "Number ninety-eight on the list." His whisper tickled her ear. The building was notoriously selective—only four units came available each year, and old-money families passed apartments down through generations like heirlooms. His junior partner position at the law firm didn't help their odds; they'd need at least another two years before he'd make senior partner. "The time will pass before we know it."

Ms. Finch's heels clicked against the marble floors. "Just sign here for the application. Five years maximum on the waiting list, usually less." She tapped a manicured nail against the contract. Everyone wanted a piece of history—the building where the rich and famous lived and where a well-known film was shot, where century-old preservation rules kept every architectural detail pristine. Between the $250,000 down payment, the strict co-op board requirements demanding liquid assets triple the purchase price, and their position behind legacy families and celebrities, they'd be stretched dangerously thin. No, they wouldn't be signing today, not with Tom's promotion still unconfirmed, and their savings would be better spent, or "parked" as Tom said, elsewhere.

Elizabeth kicked off her heels in their new starter home that night—a modest colonial with good bones and a yard that backed up to a quiet cul-de-sac. She sank into their leather couch. "To our future home," she clinked her wine glass against Tom's, while cardboard moving boxes still stood stacked in corners. The mortgage was half what the condo would have cost, leaving room for the family they hoped to start.

Three years evaporated in dirty diapers and midnight feedings. "We're up to forty-two," Tom whispered over Rose's crib. Their home office had transformed into a nursery, with walls now a tinge of yellow instead of beige. The promotion was still pending, but somehow, it seemed less urgent now.

"Number twenty-seven," Ms. Finch chirped through the phone as Rose took her first steps between their coffee table and TV stand. Tom watched their daughter wobble and fall, her laugh echoing off family photos and crayon drawings taped to walls. The Anderson kids next door had become Rose's constant playmates.

"Fifteen now," Ms. Finch's voice crackled two years later. Through the kitchen window, Tom watched water droplets catch the summer light, creating tiny rainbows. His senior partnership had finally come through, bringing the salary that could now easily afford the co-op.

Elizabeth found the contract that night, yellowed and creased. "Remember how quiet it was up there?" She curled up against Tom while sitting on their porch swing. Next door, the Anderson kids shrieked in delight as their sprinkler soaked them. The sound of children playing had become the soundtrack of their lives.

"Too quiet, maybe." Tom's fingers found the paint splatter on his jeans from Rose's bedroom mural. "No room for a treehouse twenty stories up."

Rose's voice carried from her backyard castle—their old moving boxes reimagined with crayon battlements. "Daddy, come play!"

Tom reached for his phone. Ms. Finch answered on the first ring. "Remove us from the list," he said, watching Rose knight her stuffed giraffe with a cardboard sword. The condo's pristine views and marble floors couldn't compete with the messy joy they'd found here. "We're home already."

Elizabeth's arms slipped around his waist. Through their smudged kitchen window, evening light painted their small kingdom in gold—the crooked treehouse, the half-finished garden, the tire swing swaying in the breeze. There were no marble counters or floor-to-ceiling windows, just the messy, beautiful life they'd built while waiting for perfection.

That weekend, they tackled the kitchen renovation they'd been postponing. Rose handed them paintbrushes like a tiny surgeon, her face already streaked with "Sunshine Yellow." The old cabinets came down in a shower of dust and memories—ink stains marking Rose's height, scratches from Christmas cookie disasters, and a faded crayon masterpiece inside one door.

"Look what I found!" Elizabeth called, pulling a crumpled paper from behind an old cutting board. The glossy condo brochure promised luxury living and spectacular views, a piece of New York history they'd once desperately wanted to claim. Rose grabbed it and immediately folded it into a paper airplane that sailed through their kitchen's morning light.

Tom caught the plane as it nose-dived toward their scratched wooden floor. It was the same floor where Rose had learned to crawl, where they'd danced on countless Friday nights, where life had happened while they were busy waiting and planning for someday. He pinned the creased brochure to their renovation plan board, next to paint swatches and cabinet handles.

"Our very own before picture," Elizabeth laughed, smearing paint on his nose. Through their kitchen window, the Anderson kids waved, carrying popsicles and an invitation to their backyard camp-out. Rose bounced with excitement, her yellow handprints marking the wall they'd just painted.

Perfection had been there all along, hiding in the imperfections they'd learned to love.

The Waiting Ramp

James rolled his wheelchair up to the front steps of the town's historic courthouse, the same building he'd passed by every day on his way to work before the accident. Now, the wide stone stairs stood like a fortress wall, daring him to imagine entry. His hands, hardened from pushing the wheels over cracked sidewalks, rested against the rims. He had petitioned, protested, and pleaded for months. Each time, the building's owner and his team of lawyers claimed "historical preservation" exempted them from making changes. Each time, James was told to wait. And wait. And wait.

The law was on his side, he knew that. The Americans with Disabilities Act was clear, but loopholes were twisted like vines around the courthouse columns, choking any progress. His attorney had filed complaints, but court dates always stretched months ahead. "Just wait a little longer," they told him.

Waiting became his sentence. Waiting for fairness, waiting for justice, waiting for a door that would never open.

The courthouse was a symbol of his town's pride, a stone monument they boasted about on brochures and tourism boards. But for James, it was a daily reminder that he was unwelcome. Tourists took pictures on the steps, couples posed for engagement photos, an d officials gave speeches from the balcony. James could only watch from the sidewalk. Every time, he felt erased, a citizen kept outside the circle of belonging.

One cold autumn morning, James wheeled up again, not to enter, but simply to bear witness. Children laughed as they raced past him, their sneakers slapping the pavement. He smiled despite himself. The courthouse loomed above, unmoved, immovable. A janitor swept the steps with the rhythm of someone used to seeing him there, but never speaking. James parked his chair at the edge of the sidewalk and waited. Not for a miracle, but for the dignity he refused to surrender.

He thought of the life he once had, walking up those steps with confidence, carrying files for his government job, nodding to colleagues. That version of him seemed like someone else now, someone he'd known in a dream. The accident had taken his legs, but it had also stripped away something more subtle: the casual assumption of belonging. Now, every building was a test. Every doorway asked a question: Will they let you in? And too often, the answer was no.

Inside, Edward Harland, the wealthy owner of the courthouse building, reviewed contracts with his attorneys. He dismissed the petitions with a flick of his pen, his voice smooth with confidence.

"Preservation," he said again, like a shield. "We can't alter the structure. The law won't force us."

His lawyers nodded, earning their fees by cloaking injustice in legal fabric. For Edward, it wasn't personal. It was property. Just another victory. Another man waiting outside was no concern of his. James's friends urged him to stop going, to save his strength. But James insisted his presence mattered.

Even if he never crossed the threshold, his waiting was its own form of protest. Sometimes he brought a book. Sometimes he brought coffee. Most often, he just sat, watching the seasons change—spring flowers climbing the wrought-iron fence, autumn leaves scattering down the steps, winter snow piling high against the stone. The building aged around him, and still he waited.

He thought of his mother's words, spoken often when his father was late coming home from long shifts: "We all wait in life, son. But some waits carry meaning. Yours does." James held onto that as fuel, sitting in the chill wind that ruffled his coat. His watch ticked, minutes dripping like rain down stone steps. He imagined each tick as a hammer blow against injustice, slow but steady.

Weeks later, the town buzzed with gossip. Edward's six-year-old daughter, Clara, had collapsed in the schoolyard. Diagnosis: a rare neurological illness. Permanent paralysis. Wheelchair bound. The news spread faster than sympathy could keep up. Edward disappeared from public life, his arrogance muted. When he finally returned, pushing Clara's small chair up those same courthouse steps, reality struck like a hammer. The stairs mocked him now. His lawyers shuffled, suggesting temporary lifts, ramps, anything—but preservation was still their defense, their prison. Clara's wide eyes looked up at her father, confused why she couldn't enter the grand building he once praised.

The irony was heavy, but James didn't rejoice. He had been waiting too long for empathy to cheapen it with gloating. That morning, as Edward stood helpless, James was already there. He hadn't planned it; his waiting had simply brought him again to the steps. Their eyes met across the divide. Edward's lips pressed into a thin line. The fortress he built was now his daughter's cage. No loophole, no lawyering, no shield of money could alter the truth: waiting for dignity had become his burden, too.

Clara fidgeted in her chair, her small hands gripping the wheels. She turned to James, curious, innocent. "Why can't we go in?" she asked her father. Edward's throat worked, but no answer came.

The lawyers, once so quick with language, fell silent. For the first time, Edward felt the weight of waiting not as a strategic delay, but as an ache. He saw his daughter's disappointment, her exclusion, her long wait for fairness.

James leaned forward slightly, his voice steady. "It's because some doors only open when people decide to see us." He didn't mean it cruelly. It was the plain truth. Clara nodded slowly, as if she understood.

Edward closed his eyes for a moment, shame folding him inward.

The weeks that followed were a blur of petitions reversed, funds allocated, and construction plans drawn hastily. Edward, once a barrier, now became an advocate. He attended meetings, not as a landlord defending his rights, but as a father demanding his daughter's. The very attorneys who had argued against James now found themselves drafting blueprints for accessibility. James watched it all unfold, the waiting finally moving toward action.

And James knew the deeper truth: justice delayed was justice denied. His months of waiting had carved into him a patience laced with anger, a scar that wouldn't vanish. Still, when the first section of ramp was poured, he allowed himself a rare smile. Not for Edward's transformation, not for the lawyers' about-face, but for Clara—who would never again have to wait outside, wondering if she belonged.

On the day the ramp opened, a crowd gathered. Some came for ceremony, some for curiosity. James wheeled himself to the base, placing his hands on the rims. He looked at Clara, who sat beside him, her small chair gleaming. "Ready?" he asked. She grinned, the kind of grin only a child can manage in the face of change. Together, they rolled upward, the incline gentle but steady. Edward stood behind, hands trembling on the push handles, humbled beyond words.

At the top, James paused. The courthouse doors, heavy oak and brass, loomed before them. New automatic door openers would easily send the signals for their opening, and it was done. He let his hand rest on the push panel for a moment, feeling the cool metal against his palm. He thought of every hour he had waited, every winter wind that bit into his skin, every petition ignored. He thought of the people who would come after him, strangers he would never know, who would find this ramp already waiting for them.

James didn't smile at the irony, nor did he linger in anger. He only opened the door, watching as Clara entered first. She rolled through, her laughter echoing in the chamber beyond. James followed, the sound of his wheels against polished stone a rhythm of belonging.

For the first time, he was not waiting. And neither was she.

Under the Streetlight

They gathered as they always did—seven o'clock sharp, after the last blush of sunset drained from the sky. The lamppost on the corner of Walnut and Third flickered to life, humming faintly before spilling its cone of yellow light across the cracked pavement.

"Still standing," muttered Eddie, who leaned on his cane like it was an extension of his leg. "Better than me, anyway."

The others chuckled, each with their own small sigh of recognition. Harold, whose belly had overtaken his belt years ago, lit his pipe. Dolores adjusted the shawl on her shoulders, though the evening was warm. And Ruth, always punctual, tapped her wristwatch and teased, "Late again, Marcy?" when Marcy shuffled into view.

This had been their ritual for nearly fifty years. Night after night in summer, they met beneath the streetlight where their laughter had once rung out as teenagers. They'd shared cigarettes, stolen kisses, whispered secrets, and planned futures on this very corner. But there had always been one shadow among them—Tommy, the boy who never came back.

It had been the summer of 1967. He told them he was heading home for supper and disappeared somewhere between here and his front porch. No one had seen him again. Not alive, not in the papers, not even in rumor. It was as if the night had swallowed him whole.

Yet they waited. Year after year, they came back. At first out of hope, then out of loyalty, and finally, perhaps, out of habit. But even habit carries meaning when repeated often enough—it becomes a lifeline.

"I still say," Dolores murmured, "if he walked up right now, none of us would be surprised. It'd feel like he was only gone a day."

Eddie shook his head. "He'd be seventy-four. Doubt we'd recognize him."

"You don't understand," Dolores said. "It wouldn't matter how he looked. We'd know."

The conversation drifted the way it always did—old jokes, old aches, old memories like coins they kept turning over in their pockets. But that night, the air felt different. Restless. A breeze stirred the trees in a way that made Ruth glance toward the dark end of the block, as if expecting something to emerge.

And then he did.

A man approached slowly, his gait uneven, as though testing ground he hadn't walked in years. His jacket was worn, his hat low, and a gray beard covered much of his face. But his eyes—when the lamplight caught them—were blue, the same piercing blue they remembered from summer nights when they were sixteen.

"Evening," the man said, his voice gravelly, uncertain.

Eddie's cane slipped from his hand. Harold's pipe fell to the ground. Dolores gasped. Ruth whispered, "Tommy?"

The man stopped just at the edge of the circle of light. He looked at each of them in turn, his lips working before sound came. "I wasn't sure you'd still be here."

It took a long moment before Marcy stepped forward. "Fifty years, Tommy. And here you are."

His story spilled out slowly, haltingly, like a river dammed too long. He had left home that night, restless and angry after a fight with his father. He'd caught a ride west, chasing the idea of freedom. There had been hard years—homeless shelters, odd jobs, wrong towns, wrong people. Then there was the silence of shame. How could he ever walk back after so long, after leaving everyone to wonder?

But lately, as the years pressed heavier, he found himself pulled by memory. He thought of the laughter under the streetlight, the feeling that he had belonged somewhere once. And so he came back, unsure if anyone would even recognize him, unsure if anyone would care.

For a long time, no one spoke. Then Ruth, who had always been the fiercest among them, walked straight to him and put her arms around his neck. "You damn fool," she said, her voice breaking. "We've been waiting."

And just like that, the others joined. Eddie's grip was shaky but strong around his shoulder. Dolores's tears wet his jacket. Harold muttered something about wasted time, but his own eyes shone.

They stayed together until the crickets were loud and the lamppost hummed louder still. The years between them and the boy who vanished began to soften, not erased but reshaped into something else—something that felt almost like peace.

When they finally parted that night, Ruth spoke for all of them: "Tomorrow, same place. No more waiting for ghosts. Only for you."

Tommy nodded, eyes brimming. "I'll be here. I promise."

And under the streetlight, where memory had once been a burden, it became a beacon. What had been lost was not found in the same form, but it was found all the same. And in that, there was a resolution neither time nor absence could deny: that friendship, once planted, can survive even the longest shadow.

Save the Print

The men in their stiff overalls and heavy boots move furniture around like ice cubes in a glass, not worrying about any damage. The door is fully open, and the sounds echo through the building as if a human storm has invaded and seized control of everything. The only things remaining will be the four walls, a torn rug, and a framed piece of paper.

"Is everything allowed? It's all going?"

"Everything is good, apart from that item on the wall," the man says. A dresser almost hits a man's leg, prompting him to yell, "Hey, be careful!"

The furniture poses a challenge, as it is from a time when it was made of all solid wood and not compressed fiberboard held together by small metal plugs. "We're not getting paid enough for this and for me to break a leg." He kicks the old chest of drawers and the memories inside seep out like a scent long forgotten. Now the air is perfumed for a moment and the men stop as though stricken. No, impossible, they think. It's just something left over from the old lady who lived here.

Pushing the offending heavy furniture towards the door, his partner grunts in response. "Just get it done. We've got three more rooms to clear out."

Arms crossed and with an angry expression, the man observes the chaos, the yelling, and the profanity-laden commotion. He's been present as this type of scene has played out before. Tenants come and go, leaving behind their unwanted possessions and unpaid rent. He notices financial gains on certain occasions, but not in this case. There will be no financial gain, but he will save something more precious.

The driver approaches the man, wiping sweat from his brow. Everything has been removed from the room except for one small framed photograph on the floral-papered wall. "Why is that thing considered special?" the worker inquires, gesturing and pointing his hand toward the frame on the wall.

The man's eyes drift to the object, and a wistful smile curls the corners of his mouth. "It was my mother's favorite photo of her parents when they came from Europe. She always said it brought her luck."

Now, there's a finality to it all, and the one thing that will remain is this simple framed daguerreotype, a photo actually bought at a flea market so many years ago that the man can't even remember when his mother bought it. But she scraped a few dollars together and brought it to its new home, refusing to believe it wasn't her parents.

The driver shrugs, unimpressed. "Luck, huh? Didn't seem to do much for the last tenant." Unaware that he is talking about the man's mother, he goes on with his work, strapping large pieces to his back or shoving them onto a dolly. The job is exhausting, and they've got to finish; another job is waiting for them. Who cares if something gets a bump or two? It's old stuff, anyway, and the lady who owned it is now gone forever. He thinks to himself that she'll never know now.

The man's smile fades, and he turns back to the driver. "Just make sure it doesn't get damaged. No, wait, I'll take care of it myself."

As the men continue their backbreaking work, struggling to lift the heavy, carved dining room table and solid wooden chairs, the man carefully removes the photo from the wall, cradling it in his arms like a precious child. He runs his fingers over the dusty glass, tracing the intricate lines of the artwork.

"Hey, boss!" one man calls out. "We're all done here. Are you ready to move on to the next room?"

The man nods, tucking the frame under his arm. "Yeah, let's go." There's no time for sentiment today. Everything's got to go for the new tenants who are moving in tomorrow.

As the men thread their way down the narrow, dimly lit hallway, the driver stands beside the man. "You know, I've been doing this job for a long time," he says. "And I've seen no one hold on to something like that." His face is one of dismay, with raised eyebrows and a slightly agape mouth.

The man smiles a bit less this time. "Sometimes, the little things matter most," he offered. "This photo reminds me of my mother and our good times together, and to me, it's not another piece of paper—it's a keepsake."

The driver nods, understanding at last dawning on him and changing the look on his face. "I guess we all have something like that, huh? Something that keeps us going, even when times are tough."

The man pats the driver on his solidly muscled shoulder, a gesture of camaraderie. "Exactly. And who knows? Maybe this print will bring me luck, too."

As they enter the next room, ready to start the process again, the man holds the print close to his heart. To anyone else, it may not hold much value, but to him, it's a priceless treasure—a reminder of the love and memories that can never be taken away.

Lessons From 2A

Marie's knuckles whiten as she struggles to pull at the cart's plastic handle. The wheels catch on the concrete lip of the doorway, jamming in protest. One more pull—just one more. Pain shoots through her shoulder from the weight of the groceries—milk, bread, and those oranges Harold used to love.

The first door looms ahead, its polished glass panel reflecting the late afternoon sun. The cart jerks forward and back like a stubborn mule. A bag of potatoes and that economy pack of paper towels seemed manageable in the store.

Her breath comes in short puffs now. A bead of sweat trails down her temple, catching in the creases around her eyes. Eighty years of gravity weigh on her bones.

The sound of heels clicking from behind stops. Help is coming. Marie turns, the thank-you already forming on her tongue. Shirley, in her business suit and with her practiced smile, eyes Marie for a fraction of a second before her eyes slide away like water off glass. She veers left toward the mailboxes, her manicured fingers working the tiny key into the lock.

The cart rocks precariously. A single orange escapes, rolling across the floor as though it had a mission. Marie watches it spin to a stop at Shirley's feet.

The younger woman stiffens her shoulders. With a decisive click, she closes her mailbox and strides toward the elevator, the orange a forgotten planet in her orbit.

Now, Marie's arm muscles tremble from the effort of pulling the cart. It seems to grow heavier with each passing moment as if filled with all the invisible weights of aging—the empty apartment upstairs, the silence at breakfast, the children too busy to call.

She closes her eyes, gathering what strength remains. When she opens them again, a small hand presses the orange back into hers.

"My mother says I'm the best helper in the whole building," a voice pipes up. Marie looks down to find Tommy from 2A, gap-toothed and grinning, his other hand already pulling the cart through the door.

"Sometimes grown-ups forget," he adds wisely, "but I never do."

Behind them, Shirley stands frozen by the elevator, watching the unlikely pair enter. The little boy chatters about his day at school, and the old woman nods as if each word were precious gold.

Meanwhile, the orange sits like a miniature sun waiting to rise in Marie's pocket.

Now, Marie guides Tommy to her apartment, his small hands still gripping the cart handle. In her kitchen, sunlight streams through lace curtains, casting patterns across the worn linoleum.

"We have a bake sale at school tomorrow," Tommy blurts out, scuffing his shoe against the floor. "Mom tried three times, but the cupcakes kept sinking in the middle. She says we'll have to buy from the store, but everyone will know."

Marie's fingers are still on the orange. "Store-bought?" she clicks her tongue. "Not when you have a friend who once baked for the governor's mansion."

Tommy's eyes widen. "You did?"

"These hands remember." She pulls a tin box from an upper cupboard shelf, dust dancing in the sunlight. Inside, yellowed recipe cards nestle like precious gems. "Your mother—she works late, yes?"

Tommy nods.

"Here's what we'll do." She selects a card, its corners bent from years of use. "Orange-cream dream cupcakes. My secret weapon. First, we wake up the orange oils." Plucking an orange from her shopping bag, she guides her hands to roll the fruit against the counter, pressing just enough, as her expertise has taught her.

The citrus perfume rises between them. "Smell that? That's how you know the magic's starting."

Tommy's face scrunches in concentration as he takes the orange and mimics her motion. "Like this?" Wide-eyed, he looks up at her, waiting for her answer.

"Perfect. Now, very important—we zest before we juice. But here's the real secret." She leans close, her voice dropping to a conspiratorial level. "Two drops of pure vanilla extract in the frosting and three—exactly three—tablespoons of orange juice in the batter. Not two, not four. That's what makes them dance on tongues."

Tommy hurriedly scribbles the recipe in his school notebook, tongue poking out as he writes. "Mom gets home at seven."

"Just enough time," Marie says, tucking an extra recipe card into his backpack. "Tomorrow, your cupcakes will tell their own story."

Second Chance

The hospital wall clock made a deafening sound, which seemed to ridicule the faint breathing noises that came from David's chest. Clocks are like evil specters that sit waiting on walls, their presence unnerving as they count off the minutes of our lives. Were they in competition? Medical equipment, tubes, monitors, and antiseptic odors became his world. Resting in a small bed while his bony ribs pressed against his tight skin, he anticipated the phone call that would determine everything: life or death.

Every transplant patient discovers the contradictory nature of organ transplantation; one heart beats while one stops. What would it be for him, and when would it come? The passing days melted into one another, as David found himself unable to push the idea from his mind. Somewhere out there, a patient was lying in a room surrounded by loved ones who were waiting for the inevitable. As they wait and plan the final trip, David hopes that it will happen soon. How could he possibly wish for someone to die? It hadn't occurred to him before because all he knew was there was something that would save his life, and where that something came from never crossed his mind. Yes, they said transplant, but he assumed there would be some kind of bank where they kept spare parts. The thought made him almost laugh, but he stopped himself.

Mara sat beside him while she nervously turned the hem of her sweater between her fingers. She had been his support throughout his extended period of deterioration, while her smile functioned as his only connection to life, yet it began to fade. "They said your numbers are stable," she almost chirped. Too brightly, yes, too brightly. But she was trying.

David spoke in an almost inaudible tone when he said, "Stable doesn't mean good." His voice came out as a whisper from a man with a death sentence hanging over his head. He shut his eyes before finishing his statement with a bit of gallows humor. "It means not dead yet."

Mara took his warm, pale, dry hand. "Don't talk like that." Fear wasn't something she was going to allow to mar her unmarked face. Everything she had ever been taught was now coming into play as she imagined. But it was so hard. Tears were refused exit, and the smile she wore had been practiced before she came to the hospital today. "Prepare," she told herself in a commanding voice she hadn't heard herself use. The mirror reflected back what she wished and commanded, and she was ready.

Tonight, she would be remaining in his room, as she had done so often before. A slightly uncomfortable reclining chair and a hospital blanket were all she needed as she waited for David to slip off into sleep. But just then, alarms ripped through the quiet night. Monitoring equipment screamed as David suddenly woke up with his chest constricted. Hurriedly, the nurses entered the room with automatic and robotic actions, concealing their sense of emergency. In a dreamlike state, David floated near unconsciousness while observing the scene as medical staff shouted orders, performed IV adjustments, and refitted his oxygen mask. It was full-on wartime now. They knew the enemy, and they knew the power of that presence, but they weren't going to allow it to win this night.

Mara appeared in disarray from the plastic recliner and her eyes displaying abject terror. She clutched his hand while a doctor bent low. "The heart failure rate in David exceeds what we first predicted." He emphasized that a transplant needed to happen right away.

David lost consciousness several times, but he remained conscious enough to hear Mara speaking through her sobbing. "Hold on. Please. Just hold on."

Time warped. Another nurse rushed into the room and, almost out of breath, she uttered the words David had been waiting to hear. "We have a match. Heart donor identified. Transport is already underway."

The world tilted. Mara covered her mouth while her face sagged in relief and a deep sigh echoed the sadness in her almost-closed eyes. David, too weak to speak, let the words sink in: A match. A chance. Someone lost their life that night. A family grieved. David would live now.

The surgical procedure became a disorienting time when he lost consciousness. The steady heartbeats inside his chest became audible to David when he regained consciousness after his hours in surgery. A powerful and unchanging rhythm of heartbeats in his chest kept beating with unending strength. His eyes welled up with tears when he wanted to touch his chest but was stopped in mid-air. The organ that the donor had given away now lived inside his chest.

Mara floated in the air while feeling drained yet she glowed with happiness as she said, "You made it. You've got a new heart." Her voice shattered when she uttered the last word. A mixture of joy and sadness was something new to her. Someone else's death now marked the pleasure that life had always been.

The healing process took time, but it was nothing short of amazing. Normal breathing and natural skin color marked the end of his hospital stay, and he found life outside. The feeling of gratitude existed together with feelings of guilt. Mara's online search led David to the obituary, which detailed the death of a twenty-seven-year-old teacher following a drunk driver's hit. Her students described her laughter and her devotion. Her parents referred to her as their "shining light." Now she was David's shining light, too.

He handled the paper with great care because he felt any creases would bring shame to her memory. Even this newspaper had a special sense now because of what it told him about the gift-giver. His very existence and happiness were tied to her family's sorrow.

David stood under the spring sun weeks later when he placed his hand on his chest to express his gratitude. His mind wandered to her relatives and her students as well as the empty chair, which had been hers in a now empty classroom. His survival was written in her absence.

Both he and Mara walked the path that led from the hospital entrance to the small park adjacent to it, where children with dogs pulled on leashes to maintain control. David watched this everyday activity with a new sense of appreciation. His heart maintained its normal beat as he considered the brief nature of his existence, which he received as a present rather than a reward for his accomplishments. Surely it was a present because he had been given the gift of life.

Mara reached out to place her hand gently on his shoulder. "What are you thinking?"

The experience had given David something new, a philosophy that he hadn't been aware of before. Now he knew that life is living on borrowed time. The time that he had now been given must also be shared to honor her memory of this gift. Turning his head in response to Mara's question, he simply smiled. And she knew.

About the Author

Dr. Patricia A. Farrell is a licensed psychologist, published author of multiple self-help books and videos, former WebMD psychologist expert/consultant, medical consultant for Social Security Disability Determinations, Alzheimer's psychiatric researcher at Mt. Sinai Medical Center (NYC), an educator who has taught at the college, graduate, and postgraduate levels, and top health writer for *Medium.com* publications. A flash fiction writer, she has had her stories published over 40 times in various magazines.

Her influence extends to the pharmaceutical and marketing industries, where she serves as a consultant and has appeared on major TV news programs in the US and abroad. In addition, Dr. Farrell provides continuing education modules for mental healthcare professionals and has contributed to USMLE medical school prep courses. She shares her knowledge through her YouTube channel and her daily contributions to **Bluesky** (@carpenter22,bsky.social). Dr. Farrell's achievements are recognized in *Who's Who in the World, Who's Who in America,* and *Who's Who in American Women.*

A member of the American Psychological Association and the SAG-AFTRA union, Dr. Farrell is a former board member of the NJ Board of Psychological Examiners, a former psychiatry preceptor at

UMDNJ, and a former board of directors member of Bergen Pines Hospital (now Bergen Regional Hospital).

Books by Patricia A. Farrell, Ph.D.

When You Can't Pour From an Empty Glass: CBT Skills for Exhausted Caregivers.

The Little Book on Learning Big Critical Thinking Skills

The Smart Kids' Survival Guide: Making Good Choices in a Confusing World

How to Be Your Own Therapist

It's Not All in Your Head: Anxiety, Depression, Mood Swings and Multiple Sclerosis

Unfiltered: Beneath the noise of our thoughts lies the true narrative of our minds

Unfiltered Again: A behind-the-scenes look at healthcare, medicine and mental health

Unfiltered Redux: Exploring uncharted depths of mind where masks fall and wisdom emerges

A Social Security Disability Psychological Claims Handbook: A simple guide to understanding your SSD claim for psychological impairments and unraveling the maze of decision-making

A Social Security Disability Psychological Claims Guidebook for Children's Benefits

The Disability Accessible US Parks in All 50 States: A Comprehensive Guide

Birding in the US NOW!: A birding guide for individuals with disabilities

Books by Dr. Patricia A. Farrell

How to Be Your Own Therapist

The Little Book on Learning Big Critical Thinking Skills

When You Can't Pour From an Empty Glass: CBT Skills for Exhausted Caregivers

It's Not All in Your Head: Anxiety, Depression, Mood Swings and Multiple Sclerosis

Unfiltered: Beneath the noise of our thoughts lies the true narrative of our minds

Unfiltered Again: A behind-the-scenes look at healthcare, medicine and mental health

Unfiltered Redux: Exploring uncharted depths of mind where masks fall and wisdom emerges

A Social Security Disability Psychological Claims Handbook: A simple guide to understanding your SSD claim for psychological impairments and unraveling the maze of decision-making

A Social Security Disability Psychological Claims Guidebook for Children's Benefits

The Disability Accessible US Parks in All 50 States: A Comprehensive Guide

Birding in the US NOW!: A birding guide for individuals with disabilities

A Special Request

I f this book has touched your heart, sparked your curiosity, or simply entertained you along the way, I'd be incredibly grateful if you could take a moment to share your thoughts with a review on Amazon or wherever you discovered this book. Your words not only help other readers find books they'll love, but they also mean the world to authors like me who pour their hearts into every page. Thank you for being part of this journey, and for helping stories find their way to the readers who need them most.

www.ingramcontent.com/pod-product-compliance
Lightning Source LLC
Chambersburg PA
CBHW030329020726
47493CB00004B/1206